The Death Rays of Ardilla

Captain W. E. Johns was born in 1893. After active service in the army, he joined the RFC in 1916 and flew bombers in France until 1918 when he was shot down, wounded and captured. After the First World War he stayed on in the RAF for some years before leaving to try his hand at journalism. He began writing stories for magazines as well and was so successful that he became a full time author. A very imaginative writer, he produced hundreds of adventure stories for children. His most famous character is 'Biggles', whose exploits fill nearly a hundred books.

Captain Johns lived for several years in Scotland – the Earth 'setting' for his space adventures – but later moved to a house at Hampton Court, where he died in 1968.

Also by Captain W. E. Johns
in Piccolo

Kings of Space
Return to Mars
Now to the Stars
To Outer Space
The Edge of Beyond

Captain W. E. Johns

The Death Rays
of Ardilla

An Interplanetary Adventure

Piccolo Books

First published 1959 by Hodder and Stoughton Ltd
This Piccolo edition published 1981 by Pan Books Ltd,
Cavaye Place, London SW10 9PG
© W. E. Johns (Publications) Ltd 1959
ISBN 0 330 26289 0
Typeset by Northumberland Press Ltd,
Gateshead, Tyne and Wear

Printed and bound in Great Britain by
Richard Clay (The Chaucer Press) Ltd, Bungay, Suffolk

Contents

1 Visitors at Glensalich   7
2 A strange tale   18
3 Petroconda   31
4 The peril strikes   41
5 Borron tells a tale   54
6 Problems and a decision   66
7 The world that died   77
8 On to Terromagna   85
9 More problems   92
10 Land of twilight   100
11 The ray   111
12 Mostly water   123
13 Rulers in feathers   132
14 The project   140
15 Zero hour   150

1 Visitors at Glensalich

The time was nearly midnight.

The silence that had persisted for some time in the library of Glensalich Castle, the remote Highland home of the wealthy and eccentric scientist-inventor Professor Lucius Brane, was broken by a tap on the door, which opened to admit the Professor's confidential butler.

The Professor looked up. 'Yes, Judkins? What is it?'

'There are two gentlemen to see you, sir.'

'Indeed? At this hour! Who are they?'

'One is Mr Vargo, of Mars, who assures me that the gentleman with him, a Mr Multavo of the planet Terromagna, is well known to you,' stated Judkins imperturbably.

The Professor dropped the book he had been reading. 'Bless my soul! Vargo, yes; but what could have brought Multavo all the way from Terromagna? Please show them in at once.'

As the butler retired, the Professor, lowered his chin and looked over his glasses at his companions, Group-Captain 'Tiger' Clinton, his son Rex, and Doctor 'Toby' Paul.

'I am always happy to see our good friends from beyond the – er – horizon, but I have an uncomfortable feeling that such a call as this, without warning, can only mean disturbing news. However, we shall soon know.' The Professor stood up to receive his guests.

Judkins returned with the visitors from space, and having shown them into the room, withdrew.

'Come in, my dear fellows,' greeted the Professor, warmly. 'This is an unexpected pleasure. Be seated and make yourselves at home.'

The Martian, Vargo Lentos, advanced and shook hands all round – a trifle awkwardly – smiling at this display of his knowledge of the Earthly custom. He was dressed in the uniform of the Minoan Remote Survey Fleet, close fitting jacket with short skirt, and cross-laced sandals. Multavo, clad in the official red and white habit of a scientist-doctor on Terromagna, followed his example.

'Where have you just come from?' inquired the Professor.

Vargo answered in his clear, thin, precise voice, 'From Mino, but we called at Mars on the way.'

'And what brings you here? We did not show the signal lights to bring you down.'

'Excuse me a moment while I get my breath,' requested Vargo. 'I still find your atmosphere heavy and your gravity tiring.' He breathed deeply and slowly.

'Not bad news, I hope?' questioned the Professor, anxiously.

'I dropped in to see if you could let me have one or two packets of tea,' answered Vargo.

'Tea!' exclaimed Rex, incredulously. 'Have you come all the way from Mars for some *tea*?'

'That was one of the reasons.' The visitor smiled apologetically. 'Your refreshing beverage has I fear the insidious quality of being habit-forming. Now, deprived of it when you are not with us, I miss it. As you know, we have no substitute.'

'We left you all we had with us at the conclusion of our last voyage,' said the Professor.

'You did, but I regret to say it has all gone,' informed Vargo sadly. 'Borron, Gator, and the rest of my crew, demanded their share, for they also have become addicts. Now Multavo has acquired a taste for what is, if I may say so without offence, one of the best things you have introduced to us from Earth.'

'Where are the others now?'

'They are with the ship, on the hill.' Vargo's luminous eyes glowed mischievously. 'We didn't want you to think there had been an invasion so I brought only Multavo to the house. He was most anxious to see you again.'

The Professor touched a bell at his elbow.

Judkins appeared.

'Please make a large pot of tea,' requested the Professor. 'And bring in all the packets of tea we have in store. Remember to order more.'

'It shall be as you say, sir.' Judkins went out.

'Had I realized that our tea had become such a necessity for you I would have signalled you down to collect a supply,' the Professor told Vargo. 'I see no reason why we shouldn't introduce the living plant to your home planetoid, although it is not unlikely that in different conditions it will change its character somewhat. No matter. The next time we visit we will bring an ample supply of the dried leaf in case the plants fail to thrive.'

'Thank you,' acknowledged Vargo.

'When you leave I'll take a large jug to the ship so that all on board can have a cup,' promised Rex. 'I'd like to see the others, anyway, while they're here.'

Judkins brought in the tray, and when everyone had been served Vargo said : 'We mustn't stay long. I know you always have a little fear that someone may see the ship.'

'That is true,' admitted the Professor.

'Why do you have that fear?' inquired Multavo, curiously.

The Professor's eyebrows went up. 'So you have learned to speak our language.'

'Yes. From Vargo, and the book of English grammar you lent him. I found it a very simple language to learn although some of the vowel sounds are a little difficult to pronounce. But you haven't answered my question.'

'I would rather our world did not know the truth – yet,' stated the Professor. 'You see, by a singular weakness in

9

popular intelligence it is customary here to call anyone who thinks on original lines a crank, a liar or a lunatic. Believe it or not, there are still people who are unable to grasp the fact that Earth is round. Proof that Earth is not the only man-occupied planet could have far-reaching results. We are not ready for that.'

'But I understood that some of your people are beginning to suspect it.'

'True, but suspicion and positive fact are not the same thing. Confirmation that there are older worlds than ours, further advanced in science, culture and philosophy, might well throw everything here into a state of confusion. Our mental hospitals are full already.'

'I understand your scientists have already succeeded in splitting the – what do you call it – atom?'

'Yes, but they have not yet learned how to use this knowledge properly. They think they are clever, and so in some respects they are; but I fear it is a case of a little knowledge being a dangerous thing, for now they are divided in their opinions as to what should be the next step, and people are alarmed that should they make a mistake they might blow the world to pieces.'

'It could happen,' said Multavo, seriously. 'Indeed, it has happened elsewhere.'

'The latest marvel is the launching of artificial satellites which will orbit the earth at what is thought to be a staggering speed of eighteen thousand miles an hour.'

Multavo smiled tolerantly. 'It would take me a long time to get back to Terromagna at that snail's pace.'

'Even so, the ordinary people cannot grasp such a figure, so how could I hope to convey to them the velocity of the ships in which we have travelled? By the way, what ship brought you here?'

'The *Tavona*. Gator still commands her,' answered Vargo. 'But now we must be going.'

'Before we go, tell me this, Professor, for I am rather puzzled,' said Multavo. 'Surely you have people here with sufficient imagination to project your own scientific development a few years?'

'A few years, perhaps, but not ten thousand, still less a hundred thousand.'

'I doubt if anyone could visualize interstellar television such as we saw on Terromagna,' put in Rex.

'You will come to that in time, for it is no more than a continuation of the knowledge you already hold,' asserted Multavo. 'To you, inventions like television, are still wonderful, but to more highly developed planets they would be commonplace. The danger of progress lies in trying to do too much at once. So it is with these bombs you are always making. Too much of your energy is being expended on engines of destruction. What you are doing can only shorten human life, if it does not end it abruptly. You are not alone in this, of course. Ardilla is behaving in much the same way, although in a different direction. Actually, that is why I happen to be here tonight.'

Vargo explained. 'Multavo wanted a holiday. He decided to take it at his old home, on Mino. Knowing the danger of approaching too near that sinister planet Ardilla he made a wide detour, but even so, the ship in which he was travelling nearly fell a victim to one of the red interceptors. Having got to Mino, where of course he met me, he is now faced with the problem of getting back to Terromagna.'

Multavo took up the story. 'I was aware of the risks. Ardilla is putting out a veritable barrage of rays. A stranger from beyond the Third Region who called on us told us that all ships in their section of the Universe have been warned to keep well clear of Ardilla. One of their ships, after sending out a signal that it was being tracked by a red stranger, failed to return to its base.'

'That nearly happened to us,' said the Professor, seriously.

'So Vargo has told me. This is causing Terromagna considerable anxiety. We are not exactly helpless, but we have no wish to be involved in an interplanetary war,' explained Multavo.

The Professor shook his head. 'It is a melancholy thought that even in the Outer Universe a civilized people can be destroyed by an unscrupulous aggressor. Thus has it been on Earth, and doubtless on other planets. Now it seems that even worlds threaten war on each other. Is it to be the fate of planets, that have learned to abhor war, to be exterminated by others who covet their land? Has anyone ever been to Ardilla – I mean, landed there?'

'Not to my knowledge,' answered Multavo.

'Has anyone offered to help you overcome this peril?'

'Who can help? What sort of help could anyone offer? The unfortunate thing is that almost everyone travelling in the Third Region must pass through the orbit of Ardilla; and that, as we now know, is to court disaster. To attack Ardilla might precipitate the enemy into our own constellation, perhaps even into your Solar System.'

'Someone should face up to this problem,' declared the Professor. 'As you all know, I am a man of peace; but to ignore a friend in need is common behaviour in the lower orders of animals, which are concerned only in their own survival regardless of what may happen to others of their kind. Civilized beings should rise above that.'

'Now wait a minute, Professor,' put in Toby, suspiciously. 'I hope you're not getting any funny notions about going to the rescue of Terromagna.'

The Professor looked at Multavo. 'What are you, personally, doing about this?'

'Frankly, nothing. Naturally, I would like to get back to Terromagna, but I hesitate to risk the lives of the men in the ship that took me to Mino. We were debating the problem with Vargo, Gator his captain and his old navigator, Borron, when word came through from the Mino High Council that Vargo could make this dangerous mission if he wished. That is, if nothing was heard of the missing ship within a short time.'

The Professor frowned. 'What mission? What missing ship?' He looked at Vargo. 'You told me you came here for some tea,' he accused.

'That was true. At least, it was one of the reasons. But it is also true that I wanted to see you, perhaps for the last time, before making a voyage from which I may not return. Multavo, being with me expressed a wish to see Earth and how you lived here, so I brought him along.'

'Ah!' breathed the Professor. 'Now we are getting nearer to the root of this little jaunt. Why didn't you tell me about this proposed trip of yours at once, Vargo?'

'I had not intended to tell you and would not have done so had not Multavo – what is your expression? – let the cats out of the bags.'

'Why didn't you want me to know?' challenged the Professor, reproachfully.

'Because I was afraid you would want to come with me.'

'Well, and what was wrong with that? Don't you like us any more?'

'You know better than that. I did not see why you should risk your lives trying to help someone you do not even know. Now we had better return to the *Tavona*, to—'

'Sit still,' interrupted the Professor, sternly. 'You are not going off like that. Now we know so much we must know the rest. We might even have to come to look for you. There is no hurry. It won't be daylight for a long time yet. Have another cup of tea and tell us what you intend to do, and why.'

'Very well,' agreed Vargo, in a resigned voice. 'But please

don't feel under any obligation to—'

'We shall make our own decisions,' stated the Professor, firmly. 'Proceed.'

'The facts, which are simple, are these,' said Vargo. 'They concern a planet which we call Petroconda. It is fairly large in size, nearly as large as Mars, and although we have known of it for a long time it remains something of a mystery.'

'Where is this planet?' asked the Professor.

'In terms of space travel it is no great distance away, lying in the direction of, but beyond, Arcadia – which you have visited.'

'What's the mystery about it?'

'If I knew that, it wouldn't be a mystery. As far as climate and atmosphere are concerned it would appear to be an attractive place. The air is similar to our own so spacesuits would not be required for a landing. The climate is warm. Even the nights are temperate. There appears also to be a certain amount of plant life, the ground being almost entirely covered with a long coarse grass. There is reason to believe there is no animal life.'

'Have you been there?' asked Rex.

'No.'

'Then how do you know these details?'

'The answer to that question will arise in a moment,' replied Vargo. 'Because of its favourable geographical position it was decided recently by the High Council that a thorough survey should be made. I must make it clear that a good deal of information had been gathered by direct observation, but at the time of which I am speaking no one we know had landed there. The High Council detailed a team of four picked men of the Special Fleet to make the survey. One of these men was an old and highly valued friend of mine, by the name of Quantos. Do I make myself clear?'

'Perfectly,' replied the Professor.

'In accordance with our usual practice on such flights everything possible was provided to ensure the safety of the explorers; emergency rations, a big reserve supply of air, medical supplies, and, perhaps most important, one of our latest long-distance radio installations, both for transmitting and receiving. Not that it was thought these things would be needed. There were no known dangers, but as you know, on unknown worlds anything can happen, and the precautions I have described were really no more than our usual procedure in making such investigations. Well, the party set off.'

'And what happened to them?' prompted Rex, urgently, in his intense interest in the story.

'They arrived at Petroconda, everything having gone according to plan. Their signals were clearly received and for a while all continued to go well. Quantos described what he had seen of the place, confirming what we had believed about it having no human population, but pointing out that there might be people living on distant parts of the planet not yet visited. I won't go into the physical details of Petroconda. It is more important that I should come to the real point of the story.

'On the second day after their arrival the messages were received at the prearranged time, but later on, the same day, silence fell. A complete blackout. There was no swamping interference. Just silence. Our signal receptionists listened for hours, but not a sound came through. That did not mean that hope was abandoned because it was always possible that something had gone wrong with their transmitting equipment.'

'And so?' asked Rex. breathlessly.

'Nothing more has been heard of them. They have not returned.'

"That is bad,' said the Professor. 'Is there still a chance, do you think, that they may return?'

'Who knows? Obviously something serious must have happened or we would have heard from them. Had it been only their radio equipment that went wrong they would have returned by now.'

'Had they been confronted by some unexpected danger one would have thought there would have been time to get a message through,' said Toby. 'It is unlikely that all of them would have perished at the same moment. Surely one would stay to guard the ship.'

'That is the mystery,' Vargo agreed. 'Remember, they were all men of exceptional experience.'

'And now you are going off to find out what happened,' said the Professor, pensively.

'Someone must go. It is a point of honour with us never to abandon a ship when its position is known.'

'Have you any theory as to what might have happened?' asked Tiger.

'Of what use are theories? One can provide for contingencies only to the extent of one's knowledge, and as you are aware, on a strange world there are possibilities beyond imagination. Theories in advance of facts are usually wrong.'

There was a brief silence.

Then the Professor said: "What this all adds up to is, you are going to lead a rescue party to Petroconda, and you feel that what happened to your friend Quantos may happen to you.'

'That, exactly, is the case.'

'When do you intend to start?'

'As soon as I get back to Mino, assuming that by then Quantos has not returned.'

'Would you have any objection to our coming with you?'

Vargo hesitated. After a glance at Multavo, as much as to say this is what I said would happen, he answered: "As long as you realize this may be a fatal adventure I would welcome your company, which is always stimulating and helpful.' He went on, 'It is curious, but you men of Earth all seem to have one characteristic we do not possess. It is not easy to define, but in some way it would seem to be connected with humour. Come with me if you wish.'

The Professor considered each one of his comrades in turn. 'Well, what do you say?' he queried.

'That's okay by me,' said Tiger.

'And me,' stated Toby.

'I'm not likely to be left at home by myself,' declared Rex.

'Capital. Then that's settled,' concluded the Professor, briskly. 'As there seems to be some urgency we'd better see about getting ready. There will be plenty of time for sleep in the *Tavona*.'

'Don't forget the tea,' said Vargo, softly, with one of his rare smiles.

2 A strange tale

Accustomed as they were by now to space travel the Professor's party was soon ready, and in a little over an hour, Judkins helping with the baggage, they were hastening up the hill to the small heather-covered plateau on which landings were always made. Vargo and Multavo had gone on ahead, Vargo carrying a large jug of tea, and Multavo, the extra packets of dried leaf. They made haste because a pale streak in the sky warned them that another day was approaching, and it was always desirable to get well clear of Earth in darkness to avoid being seen by an early riser, a gamekeeper or a shepherd perhaps, on one of the nearby hills.

On this occasion the precaution failed, in a manner which, while disturbing, was not without a humorous side.

Before topping the brow of the hill which would bring them to within sight of the ship they were startled to hear an outcry from a short distance ahead. Through it could be heard a shrill treble voice shouting: 'Let me go.'

Hurrying forward through the dim light they reached the *Tavona* to find a disconcerting scene which at once explained the rumpus. Vargo and Borron were holding between them a boy who was protesting in no uncertain manner. He was about twelve years old and it did not need the kilt he wore to reveal his nationality. His rich Highland brogue was enough.

'All right. Let him go,' said the Professor quickly.

'We found him trying to creep into the ship,' explained Vargo, as the boy shook himself free and glared at his captors belligerently.

'What were you thinking of doing?' the Professor asked him.

'I thought I'd stow me awa' for a wee ridie.'

'Bless my soul!' exclaimed the Professor. 'A stowaway. What next? Couldn't you see this was a spaceship?'

'Aye. I could see that fine. I ken a flying saucer when I see one,' retorted the boy. 'I've seen yon before. I only wanted a wee bit of a ridie.'

'A wee ride, indeed. To where?'

'Och. To the Moon maybe.'

Rex turned away to hide a smile.

'What's your name?' asked the Professor.

'Donald Macdonald.'

'Where have you come from?'

'Altnahoish.'

'That's the next moor, over the hill, isn't it?'

'Aye. My father has his sheep there.'

'Then what are you doing way over here?'

'I came to watch for the saucer.'

'What made you think you'd see one here?'

'I'd seen it before, when I was hunting a fox that had been at the lambs on the low ground.'

'You'd no business to hunt foxes on my ground.'

The boy, like most of his race, was no respecter of persons. 'What sort of talk is that, mon?' he demanded. 'A fox that taks to killing lambs should be hunted on any ground. Where's he come from?' he added, pointing at Vargo.

'He's come from Mars, and we're going back with him.'

'Och-aye. I dinna ken the place. Can I come with ye?'

'No. Definitely no,' answered the Professor, firmly. 'Imagine the trouble search parties would have, looking for you when you failed to return home. If it was ever discovered what had happened we should be accused of kidnapping you. Besides, we may never come back.'

'Then ye must be daft to go.'

'Maybe, maybe,' murmured the Professor, with a twinkle in his eye. 'Now you trot along and forget what you've seen.'

'Why forget it?'

'You know what they call people who claim to have seen a flying saucer?'

'Aye, fine.'

'Well, you don't want people to call you a liar, do you?'

'They can call me what they like, mon. I can trust my eyes, can't I? Besides, now I've touched one, so I know it's true.'

'If you tell people that they may put you in a lunatic asylum,' warned the Professor, seriously.

The boy laughed scornfully at the threat. "It'd tak a guid mon to catch me.'

'Well, we can't take you with us this time,' said the Professor desperately, for the light was growing rapidly. 'Behave yourself and forget what you've seen and maybe another day we'll give you a wee ride to the Moon and back.'

'Losh! That'd be grand.'

'That's enough,' put in Tiger, sternly. 'Off you go, or you may be injured by our jets when we take off.'

The boy hesitated, and then began to back away. 'Ah weel, I guess mebbe you're richt. I'll be watching for ye another day.'

'Let us go,' the Professor told the others, quietly. 'If we wait any longer it will be light, and others may see us.'

They filed on board. The double pressure doors were closed, and in another minute the *Tavona* was rocketing skyward.

Looking down Rex caught a last glimpse of a small figure, face upturned, standing beside Judkins, watching their departure.

'That was most unfortunate,' said the Professor, when, the pressure relaxing, speech became possible. 'It would be a dreadful nuisance if that boy ran home and told others what he had seen. It might force us to change our base.'

'I'd say he'll keep his mouth shut,' opined Tiger. 'I know these Highlanders. They can be tighter than oysters when it suits them.'

'All the same I wish he hadn't seen us,' returned the Professor anxiously. 'There has been talk already, you know.'

'I suppose it was bound to happen sooner or later,' put in Toby. 'We may have been lucky that it was only a boy, and not his father with a gun, on a hill.'

Multavo spoke. 'Was that a typical specimen of an Earthboy?' he asked.

'Typical, perhaps, of this particular section of Earth, which we call the Highlands of Scotland, where the people are fearless and can be fiercely independent,' replied Tiger.

'Where do we stop first?' asked the Professor, looking at Vargo.

'We'll call at Mars for news and then go on to Mino for final instructions about Petroconda,' was the answer.

'Do you think this Petroconda and the missing ship affair has any connection wih Ardilla?'

'No. It is much too far away.'

'Talking of Ardilla,' interposed Rex, 'what is Rolto doing now? Does he still carry that grudge about Earth?'

'He may, but I think he has transferred most of his hostility to Ardilla, which he realizes is an even more dangerous neighbour.

After that the conversation waned as everyone in the ship settled down to pass the time as he felt inclined.

Rex, who was about to go to bed when Vargo and Multavo had made their unexpected entry, was soon asleep.

How long he slept he did not know, and did not trouble to find out; but when he awoke, realizing where he was, he was wide awake on the instant to see the others enjoying tea and biscuits. A glance out of the window showed that they were well on their way, for Mars was already the size of the moon. However, they still had a long way to go. Vargo handed him a cup of tea.

'I wonder what we're going to find on Petroconda,' remarked Rex presently, his thoughts reverting to the main object of their journey.

'As always with an unknown planet we must be prepared for anything,' said Vargo.

'It would be a shock if, after all, we found people there like ourselves.

'It would not be a shock to me,' stated Multavo. 'In my travels I have seen many people, so their presence on any planet where living conditions are possible has ceased to surprise me. Many are alike, although there is usually some difference in physical appearance, habits and development, according to their own particular environment, of which climate, atmosphere and gravity may be the governing factors.'

'That happens with different races of men on Earth,' said the Professor. 'For instance, some of our people have black or brown skins. Ours happens to be white. Originally, the colour was determined by the climate in which a man was born.'

'It is the same on all planets,' put in Borron. 'Usually, the brighter the light the darker the skins.'

Multavo resumed. 'Why should it be strange, as so many people on Earth seem to think, that human beings should dwell on many planets? It is natural, too, that in appearance they should be more or less alike, because that's the form most likely to survive. Forms of life that cannot keep pace with progress die out. Knowledge advances with age, and that applies to planets as well as individuals. We on Terromagna have merely made progress in ratio to the age of our planet. The same with Earth. We still have much to learn. The greatest problem of all remains to be solved.'

'And what would you call the greatest problem?' asked the Professor.

'Whatever it is that decides the duration of life. Why should some creatures live longer than others? If we knew that a man might live indefinitely.'

'Are you telling me that you believe the indefinite prolongation of a man's life to be within the bounds of possibility?'

'We do now, although at one time the chances of a man living for several hundred years did seem remote.'

'Do you mean that something has happened to cause you to change your minds?'

'Yes. Before the days of interplanetary travel every world went its own way towards the solving of the great problems common to all – as you yourselves are doing today on Earth. But once interplanetary contact became possible the resultant exchange of information sent knowledge forward in leaps and bounds, as you would say. Thus will it be with you when you divert your best brains from the manufacture of instruments of war to more useful projects.'

'I have always realized that,' declared the Professor.

'Many of the things you saw on Terromagna had their original conception on other worlds,' resumed Multavo. 'And of all the worlds we have visited none has been of greater value to us than Dacoona.'

'And where is Dacoona?'

'It is a planet in a remote section of the Third Region.'

'A long way even from Terromagna?'

'Yes, for which reason visits are seldom exchanged. But the discovery of Dacoona was a revelation to us, particularly in one respect.'

'And what was that?' asked the Professor, with intense interest.

'Apart from accidents the inhabitants never seem to die,' said Multavo, simply.

The Professor's spectacles slid to the end of his nose. 'Do you really mean that?' he questioned, incredulously.

'He's pulling our legs,' breathed Tiger.

'I never engage in an occupation so profitless,' retorted Multavo. 'You should know that by now.'

'I beg your pardon.'

'Perhaps your scepticism was natural,' conceded Multavo. 'What was disconcerting to us was the fact that the people of Dacoona, while enjoying a high degree of intelligence but still a long way behind us in medical science, should have acquired by the evolutionary process alone, such a remarkable state of longevity.'

'How long do they live?' asked Rex, in a dazed voice.

'I can't say exactly but it must be several hundred years. Of course,' went on Multavo, 'there are exceptions. I am speaking of their general expectation of life.'

'Such a length of life puts a different complexion on space travel,' asserted the Professor. 'It must be possible for them to reach the most distant part of the Universe. The brain reels at the possibilities.'

'I feel like that myself at times,' said Multavo. 'The element of surprise can be overwhelming. Strangely enough, the greatest surprises are sometimes experienced in the most unlikely places. In some of the smaller towns of Dacoona the younger members of the community cannot remember anyone dying at all; and when I say younger members I mean youths of from eighty to hundred years of age – reckoned in your time. They look like young men, as indeed, comparatively speaking, they are. If the subject of astronomy is mentioned among the older men they will recall a startling occasion when, some three hundred years ago, they witnessed a solar eclipse. That is of course a rare occurrence, but we have verified it with our records. To be precise, it happened three hundred and forty years ago. The next is not due for fifty years.'

'If they are so long dying how do they accommodate the rising population?' asked Rex.

A natural question,' answered Mutlavo. 'It is one of their big problems, although nature, as so often happens, has stepped in to help them to solve it. Their long life is offset to some extent by a lower than normal birth rate, and a rather high accident mortality, although these alone are not sufficient to maintain the desirable balance.'

'What sort of lives do they lead?' queried the Professor. 'Are they what we might call slow livers?'

'By no means. They work for the equivalent of the twenty-four hours of your day.'

'But that would give them no time for sleep!'

'They do not sleep as we do.'

'How very remarkable.' The Professor adjusted his spectacles and looked around. 'We must make an effort to see Dacoona.

'It is no use thinking about that at the moment,' said Multavo. 'Later on, perhaps.'

'But why not now?'

'You would find them asleep,' stated Multavo, evenly.

'Asleep!'

'Yes, asleep.'

Silence fell.

It was broken by Rex. 'I don't understand this. You just said they don't sleep.'

'I said they do not sleep as we do,' corrected Multavo. 'They work continuously for the equivalent of eight months of your year and sleep the remaining four. And when they are at rest they sleep so soundly that they cannot be awakened. That was why I said there was no point in going there now.'

The Professor drew a deep breath. 'Well, you certainly are a man for springing surprises, Multavo,' he said, wonderingly. 'I find this possibility of extended life fascinating, but I would have thought that our on-and-off method of working and sleeping would have been more conducive to such a desirable faculty.'

'Yes, but you must remember that their depth of sleep is much greater than ours. There is also another factor, a physical one, which our scientists believe is contributory to their longevity. They have a gland situated in the centre of the neck – here.' Multavo indicated the spot with a finger. 'We all have a depression there, but with these people it is filled by a natural gland which one can see as well as feel. It does not occur in any other people with whom we have made contact. One might call it a super-repair device. As you must know, we all have a repairing activity which is remarkably efficient, otherwise none of us would live for very long. Our complicated systems are not infallible, and when something goes wrong Nature does its best to repair the damage.'

'When Nature fails we doctors do what we can to help,' put in Toby, smiling.

'Quite so. Well, we suspect that the long life of the Dacoonians is the result of an exceptionally highly developed repairing system, which almost amounts to rejuvenation, and of this the gland of which I have spoken is the centre. While the people sleep, this gland can operate without interruption. We are not certain of this. We are anxious to find out if our theory is correct, and have in mind a series of experiments to confirm it or otherwise.'

'I am glad we came,' said Toby. 'You can imagine of what tremendous interest this is to me. But before we go any farther I would like to know how you learned all this from a people on a distant planet whose language and mode of living must be utterly different from your own?'

'I've been wondering the same thing,' interrupted Rex.

'I was coming to that,' replied Multavo. 'We have known

the people of Dacoona for some time now and we are on friendly terms with them. When we made our first landing on the planet we found an intelligent race with a civilization of its own. They were well advanced in basic technology; their towns were well built and their methods of transport progressive. In short, as a society they were much like your own; but, like you – excepting the Professor – they had no spaceships. We found it easy to establish good relations with them and close cooperation followed. It was arranged that we should send some of our scholars to learn their language and study their way of life. Thus we learned of their astonishing longevity.'

'To come back to this fantastic method of sleeping, there are still things I don't understand about it. For example, how do they manage for food while they are unconscious for months at a time?' asked Toby.

'Why do you call it fantastic?' queried Multavo. 'It is merely a different method from ours. And why not? To them, our short periods of repose are just as remarkable. But to answer your question about food I must confess that remains a secret. As far as we know they manage without food. Of course, less food than normal would be required to sustain them during their period of sleep because they would not be using up their energy in exercise. It is possible that they have something in their bodies which serves as a nutritional storage plant to see them through their long period of unconsciousness.

'As a camel uses its hump for storage in desert regions,' suggested Rex, looking at the Professor.

'A better example would be our animals that hibernate during the winter – the dormouse, and some of our bears, for instance,' returned the Professor. 'During their period of sleep they come very near to death. I have been told, with what truth I do not know, that the heartbeats of a

27

bear, towards the end of its hibernation, are as low as three a minute. The food stored in its body is just enough to keep it alive until the spring.'

'Putting that aside for a moment,' went on Rex, 'What happens to the public services while the people are asleep? Do they just turn everything off and hope for the best?'

'A reasonable question,' answered Multavo. 'But you are assuming that everyone sleeps at the same time. That is not quite so. One section of the community is always in reserve to take over affairs. Moreover, they do not all fall asleep at the same instant, in the middle of what they happen to be doing. There is a certain amount of overlap. When a man feels lassitude creeping over him he makes the necessary preparations for his sleep.'

'What you might call a shift arrangement on a grand scale,' put in Tiger, practically.

'Well, that is how things are done on Dacoona,' said Multavo. 'Certainly it is an ideal scheme for preventing wars, for the whole system depends upon mutual trust.'

'But this means if we went there now we should not find *everyone* asleep,' the Professor pointed out.

'Strictly speaking that is correct,' agreed Multavo. 'When I said you would find them asleep I meant the really important people, those with whom we have made close contact. I'm sorry; I should have made that clear. I meant that a visit at this time would hardly be worth the long journey involved.'

Vargo stepped in. 'I understand that your chief research work now, on Terromagna, is concentrated on the prolongation of life.'

'Yes. Our present expectation of life is about a hundred and twenty-five years. Now that we know from Dacoona that it is possible to live longer we must learn what causes it or how it is achieved.'

'How will you go about that?' inquired Toby, whose

interest was of course professional.

'We shall shortly have the material on which to begin our experiments,' replied Multavo. 'Some scientists on Dacoona have expressed a wish to visit Terromagna, when their current rest period comes to an end. We shall teach them all we know. In return, they will allow us to perform minor operations on them for the purpose of extracting some of their glandular secretions.'

Tiger spoke again. 'Is there any point in living for hundreds of years?'

'Why not, if one is healthy in mind and body?'

'There are people on Earth who have health and wealth, which is everything, yet profess to be bored with life,' said Rex.

'Then they must be unhealthy in mind,' declared Multavo. 'Boredom is a state of mental tension. It arises from doing nothing. The brain was intended for work. It *must* work. If it is not given constructive work to do it recoils upon itself. All it does then is build up tension which you call boredom, which is a disease.'

'But surely character and will-power have something to do with it?'

'Of course; but they are products of a healthy mind. Unhealthy minds alternate between ecstatic delight and abysmal despair. It is like a road that goes up and down hills. You do not get as far in a given time as if you were moving over level ground. So the great thing is to acquire a level happiness without the depressing reverses which occur in a mind not properly balanced. You will not find boredom on Terromagna, for which reason we have no word for it in our language.'

'It seems that apart from your scientific marvels you have developed a wonderful philosophy of life,' said the Professor, reaching for a caramel.

'We are seekers of truth,' answered Multavo, simply.

'When we find it we shall pass it on to more backward planets. After all, what else is there to pass on? Space travel is a means to that end. It is only a question of time. Time inevitably means progress.'

'Not always,' said Borron.

'What else can happen?' asked the Professor.

'Some worlds die.'

'For what reason? A great catastrophe?'

'No, the human race just dies out. I have seen it happen.'

'You must tell us about it one day,' asserted the Professor.

'But not now,' ordered Vargo. 'We must return to more practical matters, for as you can see, we are approaching Mars, our first port of call.'

3 Petroconda

The *Tavona* did not stay long on Mars, for no news of importance was found there and Vargo was anxious to push on with his rescue assignment, provided the missing ship had not returned to Mino in his absence. He only made the call on Mars because it did not take the *Tavona* far off its course.

Nevertheless, the Professor and his party were allowed a little time for a short tour of inspection to see how well the work of restoration was going. With more and more families coming from Mino it was proceeding faster than they could have imagined, considering the state the planet was in when they had first set foot on it.

With the reopening of the irrigation canals and the elimination of the insect menace it was well on the way to becoming a normal inhabited planet, and Vargo predicted that the time was not far distant when all those who had been marooned on distant planetoids, by the explosion of nearby Kraka, would be returning to the home of their ancestors. Mars, as Vargo assured them, and indeed, as they were able to confirm, was still regaining its lost atmosphere, although whether this was coming out of the ground, or being gathered from detached air masses in space, was still not known. Light clouds, of sufficient density to precipitate a little rain, occurred with increasing frequency. Some of the crops, from imported seed, springing from ground that had for so long been sterile, were magnificent.

Rex rather expected to find Rolto there, the man who had a bee in his bonnet about Earth being a danger to everyone in the Solar System; but he learned that he had now returned to Mino.

The *Tavona* proceeded on its way there, Mino being the major planetoid that was its base. It was learned at once that the missing ship had not returned from its survey flight to Petroconda, whereupon Vargo announced his intention of proceeding with his rescue mission forthwith. Rex managed to have a few words with his friend, Morino, and the Professor paid a courtesy call to the High Council. Then, as there was no longer any reason for delay, goodbyes were said, and the *Tavona*, to Morino's distress, prepared to take off at once on its venture into the unknown.

Multavo found himself in a quandry. The Terromagna ship that had brought him to Mino was still there, awaiting orders. Naturally, the crew was anxious to return home, but hesitated to face the ray barrage being put up by the sinister planet Ardilla, through which they would have to pass. There were plenty of rumours about what was happening in that Region, but no reliable information apart from what they already knew. Inquiries were being made at Ando and other 'advanced' planets, and Rolto was one of those who had gone off on a search for news.

Multavo's problem was whether to risk disaster from Ardilla by trying to get to Terromagna, or wait for definite news; in which case, he said, rather than sit doing nothing on Mino he might as well, as a matter of interest and experience, accompany the *Tavona* on its rescue assignment which, if successful, should not take long. In the end he decided to do this.

The Professor's opinion of the situation was that it was not much use waiting for news, anyway, because any ship venturing close enough to Ardilla to learn the facts about what that planet was doing, was unlikely to return.

'Something will have to be done about this,' he concluded. 'If Ardilla extends its field of influence, and that is the way of all aggressors, space travel will not be safe for anyone. We still have no idea of how many ships, unknown to us, have fallen victim to these monstrous people. But for Tiger's foresight we should never have returned from our last voyage, when we were attacked by one of Ardilla's red ships.'

The *Tavona* sped on its course for its objective, the mystery planet Petroconda.

After a little while, as they gazed through the window at the myriads of stars in view Tiger spoke: 'There is this to be said for astro exploration. Men will never be without new worlds to conquer.'

'I don't like that word conquer,' protested the Professor, frowning.

'I meant conquer as one talks of conquering Mount Everest, or one of the Poles,' explained Tiger. 'Perhaps I should have said visit.'

'That's better.'

'Bearing in mind that every one presents new and unknown perils it becomes a question of how many a man can explore before he meets disaster,' observed Vargo. 'Our present journey is a case in point. No doubt we shall arrive at Petroconda, but our departure from that planet is not so certain.'

'Why do you say that?' asked Rex.

'Others have been there. None has returned. It may be that our disaster awaits us there.'

'That's a cheerful remark, I must say,' returned Rex. 'Have you no idea at all why your friend Quantos failed to return?'

'None.'

'Well, we know there is a danger so at least we are prepared,' put in Toby, philosophically.

'The problem of space exploration is that one can never be prepared for dangers that are unknown, perhaps not even understood.'

33

'I'd call that the fascination of it,' asserted the Professor, passing round his bag of caramels.

'As I have told you, Quantos and his companions were men specially selected for the mission on account of their experience. They were equipped for any eventuality within the limits of our knowledge. Yet they have not returned. I am sad for Quantos. He was my friend. I was teaching him to speak English when he went away, so that he could tell you some of his adventures.'

Borron the navigator stepped in. 'There may be difficulty in finding the exact spot where he landed. We know where he intended to land because that was worked out before the flight started. We also know that he arrived there, because he reported in his first signal that the spot had turned out to be perfect for his purpose. Nevertheless, a ship is a small object to look for on a world as large as Petroconda.'

'It may no longer be there,' said Rex.

'Had it left, assuming its radio transmitter to be in order, Quantos would have said so.'

Vargo came back into the conversation. 'All we can do is start the search at the spot where we know the ship landed.' He indicated a planet, growing in magnitude, ahead of them. 'There is Petroconda, so we should soon know the answers to our questions.'

'It looks harmless enough,' opined Rex.

'So do they all,' said Multavo, with a wry smile.

Rex, who had the 'butterflies in the tummy' feeling that always came over him when approaching a new world, said no more.

As more time passed all interest became focused on the planet on which they intended to land. By the time they were within its atmosphere, approaching from the sunlit side, they could form an idea of its surface, which appeared to be flat without physical features of any sort, and was of a monotonous greenish colour. The interest quickened as the *Tavona's* jet brakes came into action to check its fall preparatory to landing. Soon they were low enough to search for the missing ship, but could see no sign of it. Still losing altitude, Gator, at the controls, began to cover the ground in widening circles at Vargo's request.

'Never before have I seen a planet that size without even a landscape to offer,' observed the Professor.

'It all looks alike to me,' said Rex.

'That is its peculiarity,' stated Vargo. 'Every planet has its own particular features.'

'This one seems to have none at all,' remarked Tiger. 'Except,' he added, 'that the whole place appears to be covered with a vegetable growth of some sort.'

'It is all grass. There is no population, human or otherwise,' reminded Vargo. 'That is how Quantos reported the place in his early signals. In the last we had he said they were going to confirm it.'

'The place looks completely and utterly dead to me,' declared Tiger.

'There must be *something* there to prevent Quantos from leaving, otherwise he would have returned,' Vargo pointed out.

'How are we going to find out what it is, or was?'

'There is only one way. We must land.'

'Well, that's one way of finding out,' murmured Toby.

'Like walking into a lion's den to see if the lion is at home,' said Rex, trying to strike a cheerful note. 'There's the ship!' he exclaimed excitedly. 'I can see it. There it is.' He pointed.

'Yes, that is the ship,' confirmed Vargo, in his usual flat voice.

'It does not appear to be damaged,' observed the Professor, looking through his spy-glass.

'The crew are not there or they would have shown themselves to us by now,' said Borron.

'They may not be able to do that,' returned Vargo, meaningly. 'Go on down, Gator. Land as near as you can to the ship.'

The *Tavona* descended slowly, presently to put down its feet close to the missing ship, in what turned out to be a rather coarse grass about two feet high.

'By gosh! It's warm here, anyway,' remarked Rex, while Vargo made the usual atmospheric and habitation tests before opening the doors.

'As Quantos reported, the air is good, but hot and humid,' stated Vargo. 'Pressure and gravity rather less than Mars. Spacesuits will not be needed.'

'That's one good thing, anyway,' said Rex with relief.

Vargo opened the exit doors, and after a cautious look round stepped down.

Rex followed and gazed about him. Although the scene presented was as it had been described by Quantos, and, indeed, as they had observed from their overhead survey, it was with astonishment that he looked out over an endless sea of grass. On all sides it was the same, apparently a flat, grass-covered plain. The air was absolutely still. Nothing moved, not even the grass. The air was hot and felt damp, with a smell of stagnation in it. Clearly, they were in an ocean, an ocean of grass, an ocean without a ripple on its surface.

'Well, there's some good grazing here, if nothing else,' said Tiger, cheerfully.

'Because, obviously, there are no animals to graze it off,' the Professor pointed out. 'How very strange. The ground must be fertile or this grass wouldn't grow. Why, we may ask, is there nothing here? Not an animal, a bird, a reptile, or even an insect, as far as I can see.'

'There can be only one answer to that,' said Vargo, seriously. 'There is something bad about the place. We must be careful, and not let this silent emptiness deceive us.'

Followed by the others he strode toward the lost ship. The doors were closed. He opened them, slowly, as if afraid of what he might see inside. Rex heard his indrawn breath of relief when he said, simply: 'They are not here.'

'You thought they might be inside – dead?' queried Rex.

'What else could we expect to find? The question is now, what became of them.' Vargo gazed across the weary expanse of grass, for although the sun was shining in a blue sky there was something depressing about the featureless landscape. 'They must have gone a long way,' he observed. 'Let us see if there is anything wrong with the ship.'

They went in and looked around. Everything appeared to be normal. There were no signs of a struggle. There were the remains of a meal and some outer garments had been left on the seats. But there was no clue as to why the crew had left, or why they had not returned.

It was Borron who called attention to the outer shell of the ship. There were quite a number of slight dents in it.

'They must have passed through a cloud of meteorites, was Vargo's opinion, and Borron agreed, saying it was the only explanation.

'Before we do anything else we must send a message home to notify them of our arrival,' decided Vargo. 'They will be listening. I don't suppose the equipment here is working, or Quantos would have used it. We'll test it.' So saying Vargo went back into the ship, the others waiting outside.

He came out with a perplexed expression on his face. 'The mystery deepens,' he said. 'All is in perfect order. I had no difficulty in getting through to Mino. Why, then, did they so suddenly break off communications?'

'Because they went out, and something happened to prevent them from returning,' offered Rex.

'That must be the answer. Our task now is to find them, or learn what became of them. They would not go far away; or at least one would remain to guard the ship.'

"Why did they leave the ship at all?' questioned Tiger. 'They could see all there is to see from here.'

'I doubt if we shall find the solution by standing here guessing,' said Vargo.

'If they were anywhere within miles, this side of the horizon, we should see them,' declared Rex. 'On such open ground we couldn't fail to see them.'

'One would think so – if they were on their feet. But one can never be sure.'

The Professor went into the *Tavona* and came out with his spy-glass. Standing on the top step of the ship he scrutinized the miles of motionless grass. When at length he lowered the glass all he could say was: 'I see no sign of them, or any other living creature. Here, it seems, the grass is King.'

'I'll tell you something about that,' rejoined Tiger. Whichever way they went in the grass they would leave a trail. Dash it all, you can't walk through standing grass without leaving a trail.'

'Indeed?' said Vargo, frowning as if in perplexity. 'What of ourselves? We have been walking between the two ships and have *we* left a trail?'

Silence fell. They all stared at the ground. There was not a mark. Every blade was vertical.

'Dear me! How very extraordinary,' murmured the Professor, adjusting his spectacles.

Rex stamped his foot, holding some grass flat. When he removed the foot the grass returned slowly to an upright position.

'*Well*!' breathed the Professor.

'The stuff behaves as if it were alive,' muttered Toby.

'Or made of elastic,' contributed Tiger. He looked at Vargo. 'Can you think of any way in which this could have affected Quantos?'

'No.'

'It's peculiar, but I can't see how it could possibly be harmful,' said the Professor. 'Mind you,' he went on, 'there must be some reason why the grass behaves like that. Nature doesn't play tricks for no reason.'

'Since there is no trail we shall have to manage without one,' said Vargo.

'There is a lot of ground to cover. Shall we take different direction?' Tiger put the question.

'I think it would be better if we stayed together,' decided Vargo, always cautious. 'Borron can stand on the step of the ship and watch us through the Professor's telescope. He will from there obtain a more distant view than from ground level.'

'I'll take my rifle,' said Tiger. 'That should account for anything we're likely to encounter here – not that there seems anything to encounter.'

'Perhaps,' mumured Vargo.

Thus it was agreed, and Borron, with the spy-glass, took up his position on the top step of the ship. 'I will call if there is danger,' he said.

The others, the Professor's party with Vargo and Multavo, forming a line abreast to cover as much ground as possible, set off, taking a course directly away from the door of the abandoned ship, this being the direction, it was thought, the missing men would be most likely to take.

It should be said that at the last minute Rex had declared his intention of discarding his jacket on account of the oppressive heat, but his father, pointing to the edge of a cloud that was creeping up over the horizon advised him against this, saying it might rain, as from the spongy state of the ground it often did.

Rex accepted the advice, not so much that he was afraid of getting wet as because it struck him suddenly that the lost men had done just that. They had left their space travel helmets and jackets in the ship. Was there a lesson, a warning, to be gathered from that? He didn't know, but he kept his cap and coat on.

4 The peril strikes

They continued on their way through what Rex found to be a disconcerting silence, the only sounds being an occasional remark called from one to another, and the continuous swish of their feet through the long grass. This unnatural silence was itself almost a threat; at least Rex found it so. The absence of sound had a menacing quality. Was the place really dead, he wondered, and if so, why? Why were there no insects even to provide a background, however slight, with their noises? If Petroconda was as harmless as it appeared to be why were there none, he pondered.

Only the grass appeared to be alive – very much alive. It was uncanny, every time he looked behind him, to see it rising after being trodden down. There was no trail, nothing to show it had just been walked on. He had seen many varieties of grass in his travels, plenty on his own planet, but he had never seen a species with this peculiar quality. Nature, in the process of its wonderful evolution, did nothing without a purpose. There was, he felt sure, as the Professor had suggested, a reason for this strange behaviour; but there was no indication of what it was; nor could his imagination provide a clue. He found himself almost hoping that something would happen to break the monotony of what they were doing. Anyway, it all seemed quite futile, but he realized that as Quantos was Vargo's friend the least they could do was make a search, or, as it seemed, make a pretence of searching.

Actually, the end was at hand, and it came when the Professor suddenly threw up his hands, letting out a cry in which alarm and horror were blended.

They all closed in on him at a run, and then could see what he had seen.

On the ground, half-hidden in the grass, were the bodies of three men. All were dead, and had been for some time; and what had caused their deaths was plain to see. They had suffered such terrible injuries that they might have been done to death by savages armed with spears and clubs. Their heads and faces in particular were horribly mutilated. Their shirts were bloodstained, and even their hands, which looked as though they had been used in defence, had not escaped. They did not lie close together, but a little apart in line with their ship, as if each had been running towards it when death had overtaken him.

Ashen, Rex recoiled from the horrid sight as Toby dropped on his knees beside the nearest. Toby made a swift examination and rose to his feet shaking his head.

'These poor fellows are beyond help,' he said.

'Now what about the place being dead,' muttered Tiger, grimly, as hitching his rifle he looked around suspiciously.

The Professor regarded Vargo questioningly. 'I thought you said there were four men?'

'There were four.'

'Is Quantos one of – er – these?'

'No.'

'Then where could he have gone? Where was he when these poor fellows were killed?'

Vargo shook his head. 'I don't understand it. I'm sure he couldn't have been far away.'

'In that case surely he must have seen what happened?'

Vargo held out his hands in a gesture of helplessness. Never had Rex seen him so upset. But it was understandable.

'He might have been taken prisoner,' suggested Rex.

'No.' Tiger was definite. He pointed to the bodies. 'Whoever did that was not likely to be concerned with a prisoner.'

'I have a feeling there is something devilishly evil about this place,' said the Professor.

'It certainly is a mysterious business,' declared Toby. 'These men were literally battered to death. There's no doubt whatever about that and there's no other word for it. I can't imagine how it happened. After all, there were three of them together here so it would have needed a strong force to overthrow them. As a doctor I can tell you this. Some of those injuries were inflicted after they were dead.'

'I'm afraid Quantos must have shared their fate or we should have found him in the ship. He didn't see this happen or he would have sent a message home,' observed Vargo, sadly.

'He may not have had time to send a signal,' said Rex.

'Another odd thing is,' went on Vargo, 'these men appear to have made no attempt to defend themselves. Their knives are still in their belts.'

'Yet they certainly died by violence,' repeated Toby.

'The deuce of it is, there isn't a track of any sort to give us a clue as to who or what was responsible.'

'Could they have fallen out of the ship before or after it landed?' offered Rex.

'No,' replied Toby. 'Their injuries are not consistent with a fall. The cuts on their faces, for instance. These wounds were inflicted here, some of them as I said just now, after they were dead.' He shrugged. 'Don't ask me why anyone should strike a dead man.'

'Well, it's all terribly distressing,' said the Professor, mopping his forehead, for the heat was stifling. 'But we must be practical. What can we do about it?'

'I shall look for Quantos,' answered Vargo. 'To leave here not knowing whether he is dead or alive would be on my conscience for the rest of my life. His ship, of course, must be taken home. Quantos must still be here somewhere. As his body is not with the others I think it more than likely he was the one to stay behind and guard the ship. In that case he should not be far away. Someone would certainly remain with the ship. That, as I have told you, is a standing order.'

'In that case I still can't understand why he did nothing about it,' replied Tiger.

'For some reason he was unable to.'

'Then why didn't he go home, or make a signal?'

'Again, because he was unable to. I'm afraid he is dead, but we must be sure. Let us look for him. We are in no hurry. We came here with a mystery. All we have done so far is deepen it. It must be solved.'

'I don't know about not being in a hurry but I think we should be wise to return to the ship,' put in Multavo. 'There is going to be a change in the weather. I see a storm coming.'

This remark called attention to the sky, and for a minute or so they all stood staring at it, for it was peculiar, to say the least. Engrossed as they had been with the tragedy at their feet, what was happening above had been ignored. It was purely by chance, as he said, that Multavo had raised his eyes.

The storm cloud, low on the horizon, which had been remarked earlier, was now overhead, and was still rolling on at a great speed. It was the colour of lead. And it was not alone in the sky. Others, just as menacing, were advancing swiftly from all points of the compass, so that all that remained of the blue dome of heaven was a circle, around which the clouds were pouring in, like ink spreading over blue blotting paper, to obliterate it altogether. It was plain that in a matter of minutes the blue would disappear entirely.

'How very odd,' said the Professor in a puzzled voice. 'It is not unusual for a thunderstorm to come up against the wind, but here it seems we have the extraordinary spectacle of storms coming from every direction.'

'But there is no wind,' Tiger pointed out.

'There must be plenty of wind higher up,' asserted Toby. 'Clouds couldn't move at that rate unless there was some considerable force behind them.'

'The force you speak of, wind, or turbulent air masses, or whatever it may be, appears not to know what it's doing or where it is going,' observed the Professor. 'From the way the clouds are moving they are being pushed up from all sides at the same time. Most remarkable. I never saw anything like it. It will be interesting to see the result when they all collide.

'Well, let's see it from inside the ship,' suggested Tiger, taking a practical view of the situation. 'There's no point in getting soaked. If I know anything about weather conditions it's going to rain, and when it does it will be no mere drizzle.'

"It's certainly going to do *something*,' agreed Multavo.

'I'll tell you another thing,' came back Rex. 'It's turned very cold. The temperature must have dropped twenty or thirty degrees in the last ten minutes.'

'Let's get back,' said Tiger, shortly.

With one accord they turned to retrace their steps to the ships which were something like five or six hundred yards away. At the same moment a distant cry reached their ears. They all paused to look in the direction from which it had come, which was slightly to one side of the two ships.

They made out two figures hurrying towards the *Tavona*, which happened to be the ship nearest to them. One appeared to be hopping, stumbling frequently. The other was helping him, and at the same time gesticulating wildly.

'That's Borron,' observed Tiger. 'He seems to be in a flap about something. I fancy he's trying to tell us to hurry. Who's that with him?'

'It's Quantos!' exclaimed Vargo, suddenly. 'Yes! It's Quantos! I recognize him from here.'

'He seems to be having difficulty in walking,' said Toby.

'Borron must be concerned about the weather,' rejoined the Professor.

'As if we hadn't noticed it,' murmured Rex.

Vargo replied: 'Borron wouldn't make such urgent signals without good reason. We'd better hurry.'

They resumed their march, now at a brisk pace.

'Borron keeps pointing at the sky, so it must be the storm that's worrying him,' said Rex.

'Maybe he's right, at that,' returned Tiger. 'I have a feeling that this storm, when it breaks, is going to be the grand-daddy of all storms.' He glanced up, and went on quickly: 'Great Scot! Take a look at that! Did you ever see anything like it?'

Automatically turning their eyes to the sky overhead they all came to a halt to stare at an unforgettable spectacle. The blue was now no more than a hole in the clouds. But the real phenomenon was the outer edges of it. It had become a mass of all the colours of the spectrum, coiling and recoiling upon themselves, like, as Tiger observed, a circular rainbow in convulsions.

'Fantastic,' cried the Professor. 'Let us watch this. We may never see the like of it again.'

'If we don't hurry we may never see anything again,' said Multavo, deadly serious. 'I once saw something like this, and what followed was never to be forgotten. I think we would be well advised to run.'

Impressed by his earnestness they set off again, now at a trot.

A suspicion was fast forming in Rex's mind that the fate of the dead spacemen was in some way – he knew not how – connected with what was happening above them. He said to his father, beside whom he was running: 'Could those dead men have been killed by lightning?'

'I don't think so,' answered Tiger. 'Had they been struck down by lightning there would have been signs of burning, on the grass if not on the bodies. I didn't see any. In any case I can't imagine lightning making those awful mutilations.'

With perspiration pouring down their faces, in spite of the chill that was now very noticeable, they had just reached the ship when it happened. There was a blinding flash of electric-blue light, followed within a second by such an explosion of thunder that Rex thought his eardrums had burst. He staggered under the impact. Recovering, he waited for the older men to enter the ship first. Then, even as he put his foot on the step, he received two blows, one on the head and the other on the shoulder, that sent him reeling. The cry of both pain and fear that left his lips caused Tiger, who was immediately in front of him, to turn. He, seeing what had happened, reached down, and grabbing Rex by the collar of his jacket dragged him inside.

Rex, on the floor, was vaguely conscious of the ship's doors being slammed. An instant later there came a noise as if a load of bricks had been dropped on the roof. Scrambling to his feet he staggered to the nearest window to see what was happening.

Actually, he could see very little, for visibility was practically zero. All he could see was hail, but such hail as he had never seen before. The 'stones' were pieces of ice the size of cricket balls, but not all were round. Some, with jagged edges, were like miniature icebergs. He realized at once what had hit him. He clapped his hands over his ears, for under this bombardment the noise inside the ship was beyond description. Speech in such conditions was out of the question. Looking behind him he saw the Professor making urgent signals to Gator to take off. Gator shook his head.

On the floor, his head propped up by a seat cushion, was Quantos, looking near to death, with Toby, his medical bag open beside him, giving him attention.

Rex turned back to his window, wondering if the hard shell of the ship could stand up to such a battering. It was obvious that no living creature could survive for a minute in the open, which explained, should these storms be a frequent occurrence, why there was no life on the planet. The fate of the three spacemen was no longer a mystery. They had been caught in such a storm and literally pounded to death. A lump forming on his head where one of the celestial missiles had hit him was an indication of the force behind the blow. Had he not been wearing a hat his skull might well have been fractured. In the same way his shoulder, which was aching, had been saved serious injury by his jacket.

The storm did not last long. Perhaps twenty minutes, then it ceased as quickly as it had begun, leaving behind it a silence as unnatural as the din made by the hail. Outside the scene had completely altered. What had been green was now white, with ice stretching as far as the eye could see. The ship might have been on a polar icefield.

Gator was the first to speak. 'Had I taken off, as you suggested,' he told the Professor, 'the ice would have struck us with even greater force, and perhaps punctured the ship, hard though the metal is to withstand the impact of meteorites. Now we know what made the dents in the outer skin of the other ship, which, obviously, has been through this sort of thing at least once before.'

'All I can say is, an umbrella wouldn't have been much use in that little lot,' said Tiger, cheerfully.

Vargo went to Quantos with a smile of greeting. 'We found you just in time, dear friend.' Then, to Toby: 'How is he?'

'Nothing serious,' Toby assured him. 'Just shock and

exposure. He'll soon be all right.'

Vargo turned back to Quantos. 'You know the others are dead?'

'Yes. I saw them.'

'Why did you stop the signals?'

'I was lost in the fog.'

'Fog?'

'Dense fog followed the last storm. It may happen again. Yes, I see it coming now.'

Rex glanced at his window. The glass appeared to have become opaque.

'How was it that you survived?' Vargo asked Quantos.

'I will tell you all that happened, then you will understand,' answered Quantos. 'It will not take long.'

The others gathered round to listen.

'You know that we arrived here safely, for our message was received,' began Quantos. 'The trouble came on the second day. The others went out to explore. I stayed with the ship, it being my turn to remain on guard. To that I owe my life. I could see them in the distance most of the time. Of course, as you yourselves must have seen, there was really nothing to explore, but appearances can be deceptive so it was decided to make a survey at ground level to confirm that things really were as they appeared to be.' Quantos took a sip from the cup that had been handed to him, and continued.

'The weather was warm, rather too oppressive for comfort, when the party set off, as it was when you arrived. Later it changed but there was nothing to cause alarm. The clouds that came rolling up looked evil, it must be admitted, but they were only clouds, and clouds are always to be expected where there is an atmosphere. I had been walking about outside for exercise, but suddenly finding it too cool for comfort I went into the ship to fetch my jacket. That may have saved my life. From the ship I could still see the others. I saw them stop. They looked at the sky, which by that time was doing strange things. It seemed they did not like the look of it and started to walk back. That was the last I saw of them alive, for a minute later the storm broke. Watching, it was as if everything over my head, even the sky itself, had collapsed.'

'That is how it looked to me just now,' interposed Vargo.

'Like the storm that has just passed it did not last long, but it was, I think, even more violent. Everything in the air, all the moisture, seemed to fall at the same moment, and the storm ended when there was nothing more left to fall. What a sight then met my eyes – but you yourselves have seen it. The ground was white. There was no sign of my companions. Being anxious and afraid I went to look for them. I knew exactly where they were because my eyes had been on them when the storm struck. Before I reached the spot the sun was burning hot again, fast devouring the ice, although some of the larger pieces remained, and these made walking difficult and dangerous for they rolled under my feet so that often I nearly fell.'

'If the ice was melting so fast why did you not wait for it to go entirely?' asked the Professor.

'Perhaps I should have done that, but I had only one thought in my head, which was anxiety for my friends. I still hoped they might have survived, and were perhaps buried under ice. I was still looking for them when I slipped and sprained my ankle.'

'I'm afraid you've broken it,' put in Toby.

'That came later,' said Quantos. 'Limping about I found my friends – what was left of them. It was as I feared, and I realized at once there was nothing I could do for them. My ankle was by this time very painful so I decided that all I could do was to return to the ship and send a message home reporting what had happened. The melting ice had made the place a quagmire, which made walking with my injured ankle difficult and painful. Then, as if things were not bad enough, came the fog. It was then I should have stopped, but as you will understand I was very distressed by what had happened and could think only of getting back to the ship as quickly as possible. I never reached it.'

'Which explains why we received no signal,' murmured Vargo.

'Of course. As might have been expected I lost my way in the fog; but without knowing in the least where I was I kept on walking, which was foolish; but the truth is, what with the tragedy and the pain in my foot I hardly knew what I was doing. Then came the end.' Quantos sipped again from his cup and looked around.

'You would think, looking across the open plain, that it was level,' he went on. 'It is not. There are many deep holes. They look like craters, as if Petroconda had at some time been struck by a shower of meteors. Owing to the flat nature of the terrain it is not possible to see these from ground level. I fell into one, and as I rolled down the slope I heard my ankle snap. It was then that I broke it. There I was, at the bottom of a pit, sitting in water, with steep slopes covered with the usual grass all around me. How far I was from the ship I didn't know. I tried to climb to the top to find out, but the slopes were slippery and always I fell back. I tried to pull myself up by the grass, but the ground being soft with so much water it came out by the roots. Weak and sick with the excruciating pain in my ankle, which was now very much swollen, I realized that I was a prisoner, helpless. So passed my first night. With what anxiety I looked at the sky when morning came you can imagine. Another storm would be the end of me and no one would ever know what happened.'

'Have you been in that hole ever since?' asked Vargo.

'Yes.'

'You knew I'd come to look for you.'

'Yes, but I was afraid another storm would come before you arrived. I suspect such violent visitations are a regular feature here.'

'I think so, too,' put in the Professor. 'The curious property the grass has developed, rising quickly after it has been pounded into the ground, suggests that; which in turn, means that the storms have persisted for ages, because nature does not hurry these specialized faculties.'

Quantos resumed his story. 'I saw your ship coming, and knew from the way it came down that you had seen mine. That told me roughly where it was. Picture my chagrin, knowing you were so near yet being unable to let you know where I was. It was all the more exasperating to know the ships were so close because I had thought I was much farther away. I saw the storm coming, but all I could do was shout, and keep on shouting.'

'We heard nothing,' said Vargo.

'No doubt the noise made by your feet in the grass would drown my cries.'

'I heard him,' stated Borron. He looked at Vargo. 'Naturally, for a time I thought it was you, calling to each other. Then, as you got farther away, it struck me that the shouts not only did not weaken but seemed to be coming from a different direction. Guided by the sound I walked forward to investigate, and there, at the bottom of the crater, which I didn't see until I nearly fell into it myself, was Quantos. He shouted to me to run back to the ship because the storm would kill me. I couldn't do that, leaving him there, of course, so with some difficulty I got him to the top. Then we started for the ship, shouting and making signs to you to return at once.'

'A good thing you did, otherwise we might well have been overtaken and destroyed by the ice-fall; one can hardly call it hail,' said Vargo.

'That's all,' concluded Quantos.

'How long does this fog last?' inquired Vargo.

'For some hours, gradually dispersing under the sun, but I would not think it is very thick,' opined Quantos. 'Probably no more than a blanket caused by the vaporization of so much water by a hot sun. It wouldn't stop you leaving if you wanted to go.'

'I was thinking of something else,' said Vargo.

'What?'

'Your friends – out there. We have no tool to dig a hole to bury them but I do not like the idea of leaving them where they lie, to be pulverized by this brutal ice.'

'We'd better go home and fetch a spade,' suggested Tiger. 'Now we know the danger here—'

'Quantos should be taken home at once to have his ankle properly attended to,' cut in Toby. 'Having taken him home we could return with a spade.'

'I was wondering if it was necessary for us all to go,' replied Vargo. 'We have two ships, both serviceable.'

'What have you in mind?' asked the Professor.

'Simply that the *Tavona* waits here while someone, one or two members of our crew, takes Quantos home in his own ship. It could return bringing digging implements which are not part of our usual equipment.'

'That seems a sensible arrangement,' answered the Professor. 'We have had proof that the ships can weather these storms, should another occur in the interval. I would like to examine this grass more closely.'

The matter was soon settled, it being arranged that two experienced members of the *Tavona's* crew should take the lost ship home, with Quantos. Toby insisted on going with his patient who, in spite of his protests that there was nothing wrong with him, was apart from his ankle, in a bad way, as was to be expected after what he had gone through.

Presently those who were to stay watched the other ship fade like a ghost in the mist above them.

5 Borron tells a tale

For two days the *Tavona's* company lounged about the ship doing nothing, for there was nothing to be done. Without anything to look at except the endless plain of grass, unbroken by any object to catch the eye, this soon became a boring occupation, and Rex found himself wishing he had gone with Toby to Mino, where he would at least have had the pleasure of seeing Morino.

Not a cloud appeared in the sky, much less a storm, to break the tedious monotony.

At the suggestion of the Professor, whose interest in the grass was soon satisfied, the *Tavona* took off, leaving a small pyramid of empty food containers to mark the spot, and circumnavigated the storm-flayed globe to confirm that it was the same everywhere. It was. Only the grass, which alone had adapted itself to the singular conditions – assuming that in the past there had been other forms of life – flourished, and this, unmolested, taking advantage of having a world to itself, had overrun the planet.

'Quite obviously, from what we have seen here, nothing else would have a chance of survival,' declared the Professor on their return to the marker pyramid. 'The ground appears to be fertile, but a tree in the seedling stage, should it be introduced by accident or design, would be smashed to pulp before the wood could harden.'

'The storms make the planet useless for any practical purpose,' said Vargo. 'That answers the question that caused the investigation to be made. There is, therefore, nothing more for us to do, and I, for one, shall not be sorry to see the last of a place that has not one thing to recommend it.'

There was, literally, nothing for them to do except sit

about waiting for the other ship to return with the digging implements. In transit between planets this absence of any sort of occupation was accepted because it was inevitable, but, curiously perhaps, with his feet on the ground Rex found it harder to endure.

By night there were, of course, stars all around them. That, in the nature of the Universe, was bound to be so on any planet, although the positions of the constellations were never the same. Petroconda could also boast a moon, which, it had been supposed, was merely a minor satellite. But remarking on this the Professor was informed by Borron that this was not so. The body they could see was actually a fairly large planet in its own right.

'How do you know that?' asked Tiger, filling his pipe.

'Because I have been there,' returned Borron, calmly. He went on: 'Do you remember me saying, not long ago, that civilizations do not last indefinitely? Like everything else they must eventually die. I said I was sure of that because I had seen a dying world.'

'I remember,' said the Professor.

Borron pointed to the shining orb in the sky. 'That is it,' he stated. 'I was there only once, long ago, when I was what I believe you call an apprentice in space navigation. But I remember the place well. It made a profound impression on me and I have never forgotten it. I would say that as far as human beings are concerned it is now dead.'

'That means there were people there when you called.'

'Yes, we saw quite a number of men,' confirmed Borron, in a curious tone of voice.

'Were they civilized?'

'In a way, yes. Or they certainly had been. In the fine arts, notably in painting, sculpture and architecture, they had reached a point far beyond anything I have ever seen anywhere.' Borron threw a sidelong glance at Multavo. 'And that includes Terromagna,' he added.

'But you say they were dying.'

'Yes.'

'For what reason?'

'They had to die.'

'Did they know they were going to die?'

'Yes. They were resigned to death.'

'It must have been a depressing place,' put in Rex.

'It was.'

'Were they being killed off by some disease?' questioned the Professor, his eyes bright with interest.

Borron hesitated. 'I suppose you could call it that.'

What were the people doing when you were there?'

'They were doing nothing.'

'Just waiting for death to overtake them?'

'Exactly.'

'That seems a dull way to end up,' remarked Rex.

'How else could they end up?' inquired Borron. 'Consider the circumstances. Peoples can vanish in a flash, as for instance in the case of Kraka when it exploded; the victims of that catastrophe knew nothing of it. Or they can die slowly, and that, I do assure you, for I have seen it in process, is a much more dismal fate.'

'At least the people have time to prepare for death.'

'You would think that, but in actual fact they do not. They simply wait for it. Overwhelmed by a sense of utter futility they do nothing at all. What is the point of doing anything if you know you are going to die? Imagine what would happen on our own Earth if the present generation knew the end was inevitable in the foreseeable future. All activities would stop. Without the satisfaction of achievement all incentives would vanish. Without a future nothing could have any value. Articles that had been priceless would have no worth because, when all is said and done, there is only one thing of basic value and that is life itself. Without that you have nothing.'

'What is the name of this place?' Multavo, put the question.

'We named it Selinda.'

'I seem to have heard of it,' murmured Multavo. 'I think one of the Terromagna ships once called there, but it was some time ago and I did not hear the details.'

The Professor reached for his caramels. 'As we have nothing to do, Borron, I think you might tell us more about Selinda. It would help to pass the time.'

'Do not expect a lurid story of adventure,' adjured the old navigator. 'It is a simple one of a sorrowing people who saw before them only extinction, and the dissolution of thousands, perhaps millions, of years' work by their ancestors.'

'But couldn't these wretched people escape to another planet?' asked Rex. 'Why did they stay there?'

'Having no means of transport they could not do that even if they had wished to migrate. They had no mechanical devices of any sort, their lives, and the lives of their forebears, having been devoted entirely to art. We offered to take some of the men away with us, but they declined, saying that if their time had come they would all perish together on their own ancient world. Such is the attraction of what we call home. It is something that is born in us and remains with us to death.'

'I find this fascinating,' asserted the Professor. 'Please proceed with the story.'

'Selinda, unlike some minor planetoids in the region, was known to have an atmosphere,' explained Borron. 'We could see it from Mino. No ship was known to have called there because, after all, with millions of worlds in space, to visit them all in a lifetime is not possible. But it happened that the ship on which I was learning my astronautics, one of the Outer Region Survey Fleet, was in the area, and Langor, its Commander, one of the most skilful and intrepid explorers Mino has ever produced, decided to investigate. He is dead now, but in his day he was a great man, and fearless. We owe much of our knowledge of the Universe to him. We went down. Not necessarily to land. But what we saw from a close view both surprised us and aroused our curiosity.'

'And what did you see?' asked Rex, who was following the story with intense interest.

'We saw a world of the highest order, well-furnished with vegetable and animal life. There were magnificent forests, and open plains on which grazed herds of animals, large animals of species unknown to us. Scattered about were some fine towns, with many really splendid buildings which even from above we could see were in a state of disrepair. In some places the forests appeared to have encroached, too. Around these towns were walled enclosures, suggesting cultivation on an intensive scale. But signs of what you would call human beings there were none. Naturally, we came to the conclusion that here was a world on which a highly civilized people had been destroyed by an overwhelming disaster in the not very distant past. What else could we think with not a living soul in sight?'

'You were bound to come to that conclusion,' agreed Multavo.

'Our commander decided to land in the hope of finding out what had happened, and in fact we were nearly down, stationary to make the usual habitation tests, when we saw a small group of people standing together, not in a town, but near some smaller buildings in one of the fields close by. They were watching us. We landed between them and the town so that we were no great distance from either. I was allowed to go forward with the commander and two members of the crew, and while I cannot say I have never seen a stranger picture than that presented by the inhabitants as they stood watching and waiting for us, the situation provoked the greatest curiosity.'

'In what way?' asked the Professor.

'In the general untidiness of the place, and perhaps even more by the appearance of the men. They were all dressed alike, in white robes of some rough material caught in round the waist by cords with the ends hanging loose. I say white, I should have said *had* been white, for they were now anything but clean and in some cases they were threadbare. Perhaps there was nothing particularly remarkable in that. What was odd was the way they stood in a compact group, with the exception of one very old man who sat in front on a stool, regarding us with a sort of calm indifference. In appearance they might all have been reproductions of the same man. All were aged, with long white hair and beards. They were a good-looking race, with finely cut rather delicate features, high foreheads and intelligent eyes. Yet in some strange way every face wore the same expression, which I can only describe as one of resignation or despair. They didn't move. The didn't speak. They just looked at us, showing neither friendliness nor hostility. We stopped at a distance of a few yards from them, for we were now faced with the difficulty that always arises when one meets a strange race of men for the first time.'

'Language,' murmured the Professor.

'Yes. There were many questions we would have liked to ask. What had happened? What were they doing there instead of living in the town? Where had the rest of the people gone? Why were they all old? Where were the women and children? for there was not one in sight, which was most unusual because, as you must know by now, the children are the first to run out to gaze at a visitor from space.'

'How many men were there in this group?' asked Tiger.

'I didn't count them but there must have been between forty and fifty.'

'All old?'

'Yes.'

'What sort of age?'

'Not knowing their normal life-span I wouldn't attempt to guess. Some were older than others, in case I gave the impression that they were all of exactly the same age.'

'No sign of disease or sickness?'

'No, although they looked anything but robust. Their faces were pale and lined, as if they had been through some great trouble. Our own intentions were friendly, of course. They must have known that since we carried no weapons. We were more than willing to help them, should help be needed, if it was in our power.'

'You couldn't tell them that.'

'Of course not. Langor made the usual signals, holding out his hands palms upwards to show that we came in peace. The old man returned the sign, showing small, beautifully made hands, as small and delicate as those of a girl. Langor offered a parcel of food. The old man shook his head without even glancing at the present.'

'How very disconcerting,' murmured the Professor.

'To me, at the time, the situation produced a sensation of unreality. Imagine the position. For a little while we stood there looking at each other with Langor trying to put questions with his hands. As you know, one can convey much by sign language, and our commander, being a man of great experience, was adept at it; but it is a long and laborious method of carrying on a conversation, requiring much patience. I will not bore you with details, but Langor did make himself understood fairly well. To interpret the old man's answers was much more difficult, and for a time it looked as if our curiosity would remain unsatisfied. Then one of the younger men went to the old one and said something to him. Apparently it was a suggestion, for the old man made a sign of assent. The man who had spoken then came to us, and making signs that we were to follow him set off towards the town. Wondering what we were about to see, we followed him.

'The intermediate ground was in a state of rack and ruin, and it was clear that the people had stopped cultivating their fields. Perhaps it wasn't necessary, for there was plenty of corn and fruit growing more or less wild. But when we came to the town I gasped at the beauty and quality of the architecture, although, to be sure, there was the same appearance of neglect and decay. There was not a soul in sight. The only sound was that of our feet on the road, disturbing the dust that lay on it.'

'I have never seen a completely empty town but I can imagine it is a weird experience,' said the Professor, quietly.

'It is more than that. It was frightening,' declared Borron. 'I had a feeling we were not alone; that there was somebody there, watching us, from windows, or corners. But I must tell you about the buildings. They were magnificent. Perhaps I should say beautiful, because none was of great size. They were of several colours and materials, notably of marble, white, green, blue or mottled. But it was the craftsmanship of the decorations that enchanted me. Every façade had been exquisitely carved, some with formal designs, others with figures of men, women and children, fruit or flowers. I would not hazard a guess as to how long it must have taken to design and complete these works of art. They were, I think, of great antiquity.'

'Then there could have been no storms such as we have seen here,' remarked Tiger.

'It was certainly a perfect day when I was there, warm, a blue sky above, flowering trees and shrubs all around us. What the winter there was like, or even if they had one, I do not know. There was one rather curious incident, although it has no real bearing on my story. We were passing a long, particularly striking building, made of some very dark stone, perhaps black marble. The doors were wide open, and

Langor moved as if he would enter; but our guide seized his arm and dragged him away, making very definite signs that we were not to go in.'

'So you never knew what was inside?'

'No.'

'How very annoying.'

Borron smiled. 'I've often wondered. Well, to continue, our guide had another shock for us. He took us into a long hall of pure white marble, and the reason he had done so was at once apparent. Painted on the walls, in long conspicuous strips, were pictures, the like of which I have never seen. Not only were the colours brilliant but the drawing was lifelike. Everything was perfect, down to almost microscopic detail. The scenes depicted were in sequence, and it did not need much imagination to perceive that here was the story of the planet and its people. We were at once engrossed. Our guide, clearly in no hurry, sat on a bench and awaited our pleasure. The pictures, showing a train of events, were as easy to follow as would have been writing in our own language.'

The Professor interposed. 'Apart from the high standard of workmanship, as you describe it, I can't say I'm particularly surprised, for more than one ancient race on Earth has told its story in the same way, sometimes in wall paintings, and sometimes with rock carvings in the open air. More often than not such works reveal the career of a great monarch who wanted to be sure that his prowess was known to posterity. In the country we call France there are very ancient paintings on the walls of caves.'

'The Bayeux Tapestry, two hundred and thirty feet long, tells the story of William the Conqueror's invasion and conquest of England, and that's going on for a thousand years old,' reminded Tiger. 'But go on, Borron. This is a most fascinating story. Sorry I interrupted.'

'The story of Selinda, as we made it out, was this,' resumed Borron. 'It began with a picture of the planet as it must have been at some time in the past – men working on buildings or handicrafts, animals in the fields, corn and vegetables growing, and everyone obviously happy. It was a world as near perfect as men could make it. The next pictures showed the first signs of calamity, animals lying dead, crops and trees withered, men, women and children sitting about as if they were sick.'

'Was there anything to show what had brought about this tragic state of things?'

'Nothing.'

'Why do you suppose that was omitted?'

'I can think of only one answer to that,' returned Borron. 'The people themselves did not know. The cause of the catastrophe was something outside their knowledge; something that had never happened before. Unable to do anything they could only submit. This was made clear by the final pictures of the series, which looked as if they had been done hurriedly. They might have been illustrations of a stricken battlefield, or a people struck down by some terrible plague. Men, women and children lay about, dead or dying. Some were in flight. Others watched helplessly. Nothing was being done. Everything, including buildings under construction, had been abandoned.'

'And that was the end?' breathed Rex, in a shocked voice.

'Not quite. There was a picture showing what seemed to be the start of a migration. A party of young men, with their wives and children, with loads on their backs, on the point of departure, presumably to seek another home; for next we see them in the distance. Apparently this was a success, for a similar scene shows them, returning. The men were now old, white-haired and bearded, so some time must have elapsed. That was how we read it. Behind them, in the sky, was an awful picture depicting Wrath, possibly a god of some sort. There was another significant feature. There were no women or children in the party.'

'What did you make of that?' asked the Professor.

'Langor, at the time of our visit, observed that in each successive picture the number of women shown became fewer. That, he was convinced, was not an accident or an oversight. It was deliberate, Naturally, the number of children was fewer, too. Towards the end, among the children, there was a complete absence of girls. Every child, what few there were, was a boy. The last picture, which had not been finished, showed the place very much as we ourselves saw it. A few old men were standing together, just as those had stood on our arrival. This picture, I'm sure, was intended to convey that these old men were the sole survivors of the population. That's all.'

'And what were your final conclusions about all this?' asked the Professor, after a short silence.

'We decided that the absence of women could mean only one thing. If no females were being born there could be no mothers. It seems that for some reason, for which I have no explanation to offer, the women were more susceptible to the affliction. They were the first to go, so the number of children born was bound to decrease from that time. We need not suppose that all this happened in a moment. It was probably a slow process spread over a long period. Anyway, the end was inevitable. With no women left the race was doomed to extinction. Thus, for no apparent reason, can the well-established population of a planet perish.'

'There must of course have been a reason,' asserted the Professor.

'That is beyond dispute, but we were unable to find it.'

'There was no shortage of food?'

'Not when I was there.'

'No signs of disease among the men?'

'None.'

'So you came away without solving the mystery.'

'What else could we do? I think we were all a little afraid that if we stayed there we too might become affected; which was why we hurried away and never went back.'

'Didn't you offer to take those wretched men with you?'

'Yes, but they declined. To import new people would not restore the original population. That would merely be to introduce another race, with different habits and customs, and without the artistic ability of the old one. The men we saw, the last few survivors, knew that the end was in sight, and for that reason had no interest in anything. For them there was no hope, no future, only the gulf of utter oblivion, and they had accepted what they knew to be inevitable. There was no alternative. All they could do was wait for death to take them one by one.'

Rex shook his head in sorrow. 'What a terrible prospect for the last two left alive, each wondering who would be the first to go. Imagine being the last person——'

'Don't let your imagination run away with you,' warned Tiger.

'I suppose they are dead by now so their sufferings are over,' concluded Borron.

'No one has been back to see?' questioned the Professor.

'Not to my knowledge.'

Silence fell.

6 Problems and a decision

A profound and somewhat uncomfortable hush fell in the *Tavona* when Borron finished his tragic story. It lasted for some time, the Professor polishing his spectacles reflectively, Tiger filling his pipe and Rex gazing through the open doors at the grassy world beyond.

At last the Professor said: 'Without questioning the decision of your commander, it does seem an awful thing that you had to go away leaving these miserable men to their fate.'

Borron agreed. 'What else could we do?'

'I'm thinking not only of them from the purely humanitarian angle,' went on the Professor. 'Nor am I concerned entirely with the loss to the Universe of their exceptional artistic talents, which would be a great pity. But what of the thing that destroyed them? Whatever happened to them could, we may presume, wipe out any other civilization.'

'I've often wondered what it could have been.'

'It was no use wondering after you had left, my dear fellow,' retorted the Professor. 'You owed it to the Universe to find out what it was while you were there.'

'Langor did his best, but had to admit he was baffled.'

'You didn't eat or drink anything while you were there?'

'No local food.'

'No water?'

'No. Langor placed a veto on everything.'

'He may have been wise.'

Tiger looked at the Professor. 'You have an idea?'

'Several.'

'You think it might have been something in the food or water that did the mischief?'

'It is one possibility.'

'In what way?'

'The food or water might have become contaminated.'

'But that would introduce disease, and Borron says he saw no signs of any.'

'That doesn't mean it was not present in a form unknown to him.' The Professor turned to Borron. 'That black building your guide would not allow you to enter. Did you never see inside it?'

'Not really. Only from a distance. The place appeared to be empty.'

'You couldn't identify the material used for the building?'

'We didn't try. It didn't occur to us to examine it. Why should it? It looked harmless enough. I doubt if our guide would have allowed us to go near it.'

'He acted as if he was afraid of it?'

'Yes.'

'I regard that as significant. We might almost call it a clue to the mystery. Did you notice any other buildings of the same material?'

'I can recall one, in an unfinished state, farther up the street than we went. Beside it was a big pile of the stuff, cut into cubes ready for use.'

'Did you observe the quarry, or the place from where the material was obtained?'

'No. I think it must have been brought from some distance away.' Borron suddenly knitted his forehead. 'Wait a minute. I *do* recollect something. As we made our survey from above we noticed a considerable area of devastation surrounding a small group of mountains. Much of it appeared to be sterile desert, yellow sand; but the centre was black. There was also a number of outcrops of black rock – or what we took to be outcrops.'

'You didn't investigate this?'

'No. There was no point in it. We were more interested

in the fertile part of the planet, where people, should there be any, were most likely to be found.'

'Of course.' The Professor pursed his lips.

'What's at the back of these questions?' asked Tiger.

'I'm thinking of possible contamination by radioactivity,' explained the Professor, pensively.

'What connection could that have with black rock?'

'I'm wondering if by any chance this dark stuff could have been pitchblende, or some form of it. If so, the enthusiasm of these artists for a new material on which to work may have been their downfall. As you know, pitchblende is the deposit from which, on Earth, we derive radium. It diffuses radioactivity, which is dangerous stuff to play about with. It cost the discoverers their lives. The people of Selinda would be unaware of its deadly properties until slow death began to ravage them, when they may have suspected it. By then the damage had been done. Was *that* why the people had moved out of the town? Was that why the guide kept you clear of the black building?'

'It could have been,' agreed Borron. He went on slowly. 'There was a picture showing the stuff being manhandled, cut into blocks and carved. We know there are many emanations from various substances that can affect a body in a variety of ways.'

'Exactly!' exclaimed the Professor. 'All this sounds to me like an overdose of radioactivity, for if we rule out famine and disease what else could it have been? A gas of some sort, perhaps. People do not die for no reason at all. A little while ago we were talking of the human body having a repair outfit, but it has not yet learned how to cope with the devastating effects of what, for want of a better name, we call radioactivity, or, for that matter, poison gas. One effect of it might be to prevent the birth of children. That would account for the conditions found by Borron on the occasion of his visit to Selinda. The only thing against the gas theory is that it would strike swiftly, without discriminating between men and women.'

'We suffered no ill effects,' said Borron.

'It could be that you were not there long enough. Or again, the emanations might have become exhausted.'

Rex stepped into the argument. 'The figure in the sky, in one of the pictures, which Borron said might represent the Wrath of God, suggests that the trouble came from above.'

'Very good. You make a point there, Rex,' congratulated the Professor. 'Very well. If the people didn't know what was causing the trouble they might have attributed it to the vengeance of their god. A nation so advanced would certainly have a religion of some sort. It is a common thing on Earth for savages to lay the blame for their misfortunes on their pagan gods, whose displeasure they have incurred. They try to propitiate them by sacrifices, sometimes human ones. In the case of Selinda the trouble may have dropped like rain from the sky, either by reason of a tremendous explosion on the planet itself, or somewhere in its constellation. We know that explosions on our own sun release electronic particles that affect our radio. The wretched bombs with which some of our so-called experts are amusing themselves have a fall-out of death-dealing radiation. If we can produce such a horror by artificial means why should it not happen in space?'

'But had that happened surely we should have seen signs of it,' said Borron, dubiously.

'Perhaps you did. You admit you saw an area of wide-spread devastation.'

'It was some distance away from the town.'

'What of it? This horrible affliction can be introduced into a man, woman or child, in more ways than one. For example: the murderous particles carried by the wind after an atomic explosion fall on the grass. Domestic animals eat the grass. In the case of cows' milk it can be passed on to the people who drink it. One of the by-products of fall-outs is strontium, which makes bone, and already there is a suspicion on Earth that children have more strontium in their bones than they used to in the past. Where has it come from? We may well wonder in what other ways, as yet unknown, the human body, or its organs, can be affected by particles of elemental matter floating about in space. I would very much like to test my theory about Selinda.'

Tiger frowned. 'Are you thinking of going there?'

'Why not, if we could get back in time to be here when the Doctor returns? I have a small instrument of my own, in my kit-bag, on the lines of a Geiger counter, that will tell us in a moment if Selinda is suffering from radioactive poisoning. What do you say, Gator? You are in charge of the ship. The decision must rest with you.'

Gator had a quiet conversation with Borron, at the end of which he said: 'Yes, we could go, provided we do not stay too long on Selinda. I would myself be interested to see this place. It is no great distance from here.'

'We could leave a message here for Toby, to say where we'd gone, in case our return was delayed and he was back first,' said Rex.

'Then let us go,' went on the Professor, briskly. 'Anything is better than sitting here doing nothing. If we are too late to save the artists we may still be in time to save those wonderful pictures.'

'You couldn't move them,' declared Borron. 'They are painted directly on the marble walls, polished, I think, for that purpose.'

'I could make photographic copies. What a wonderful thing it would be to have copies of works of art created on another world!' The Professor chuckled. 'If they are as good as you say they are, my dear Borron, think what a stir they would make in our own artistic circles. Think of the guesses that would be made at the name of the painter! They would set a new standard to work to.'

'You'd show them?' queried Tiger.

'Certainly. Why not? No one would guess where they came from, and if I told the truth no one would believe me.' The Professor became serious. 'I am still hoping to save these unlucky people, should any remain alive.'

'How could you do that?' Multavo asked the question.

'They must be persuaded to leave the planet. On Terromagna, for instance, they could instruct others in their art, and perhaps write the history of their planet.' The Professor became enthusiastic. 'They might even marry some of your girls, and later return to Selinda to re-establish their civilization.'

'It wouldn't be much use going back if the same destructive conditions prevailed,' stated Tiger, grimly.

'That's all the more reason why we should investigate,' declared the Professor. 'If the source of the trouble can be located it might be possible to eliminate it. If that proved to be impossible – well, that would indeed be the end of Selinda. However, it's no use making plans until we know what caused the mischief, or if anyone is left alive.'

'Then let's press on to Selinda and get the facts,' suggested Tiger. 'If we're going, let's go, and quit guessing. As an engineer there's one thing that puzzles *me*. It hasn't been mentioned yet. How were these wonderful buildings erected? What did the workmen use for tools? They'd need metal. You don't carve stone with wood. Did you see any metal, Borron, when you were there?'

'No. But we didn't look for any. We were too taken up with the people themselves. All I can say is that I saw no implements or mechanical devices of any sort.'

Tiger nodded. 'That's a mystery *I* should like to solve.'

'Metal, if left unattended, would disappear over a period of time by oxidization,' stated the Professor.

Preparations for departure were soon made. The message,

saying where they had gone, was left in the conspicuous position on the marker pyramid for Toby, and the *Tavona* once more sped away into space.

Rex picked up a book intending to read but found it less exciting than what he himself was doing. He had lately noticed more and more on his space voyages that in some strange way his normal routine at home was becoming less real than this new life among the planets. Why this should be he did not know, unless it was that knowing interstellar flight to be an established fact it absorbed his interest to the exclusion of everything else, certainly to a greater extent than anything he could have done on Earth. As for his school-days, they now seemed part of another existence, as remote as if he was looking at them through the wrong end of a telescope.

After a little while he put the book aside and, with a glance at his watch, settled down to sleep the time away.

When he awoke, having consulted his watch, which told him he had slept for nearly seven hours, he turned immediately to look at the planet and observed from its increased size that they would reach it before he would need more sleep. Seeing the Professor in quiet but earnest conversation with his father over the usual frugal meal, he joined them, to hear the Professor say: 'From Borron's description of the place, the fact that some of the plant and animal life has recovered would seem to indicate that the destructive agent, whatever it was, had died out or passed on.'

Tiger answered: 'It sounds as if everything had recovered except the human population. How could that happen?'

The Professor shook his head. 'A difficult question, my dear Group-Captain. It could be because the humans, with their complicated internal organs, were more vulnerable to the onslaught, or because they recovered too late, their numbers having fallen below the point of recovery. The same sort of thing has been known to happen on Earth to certain animal and vegetable life. It has been estimated that if anything falls to less than ten per cent of its normal numbers it becomes extinct, the reason being that its natural enemies, having once got the upper hand, maintain their supremacy. It happened to the dodo and the great auk. This trip promises to be the most interesting we have ever undertaken and we should learn something from it. That an entire people, highly intelligent, can disappear from their world, leaving their works behind them, is something I never contemplated, and provides a lesson that other worlds, including our own, would do well to keep in mind. Well, it looks as if we shall soon be at our destination.'

The Professor turned to Borron, who was sitting by Gator at the controls. 'Do you think you will be able to find the same spot on which your old commander made his landing?'

'It should not be difficult provided there has been no great change.'

'You're quite sure that was no one on Selinda apart from the people you saw?' queried Tiger.

'Almost sure,' answered Borron. 'We girdled the globe several times, quartering, at a low altitude, without seeing anyone. The area on which we landed seemed to be the most fertile part of the planet. Elsewhere, as I have said, there was much desert. That is why I doubt if we shall find anyone alive. All the men we saw were old.'

'They might have *looked* old because they all wore beards,' suggested Rex, hopefully.

"They were white.'

'That might be the natural colour of their hair.'

'Or their hair may have turned prematurely white as a result of the disorder from which apparently they suffered,' put in the Professor.

'We shall soon know, for we haven't much farther to go,' said Borron, evenly.

The *Tavona* flashed on through the great void, and a little later was close enough for those in it to get a distant view of the World without Women, as Tiger called it, jokingly, to ease the tension. It could now be seen that both hemispheres were in daylight, one side brighter than the other, as a result of having two suns, one larger and therefore presumably nearer, than the other.

'This is a strange thing,' said Borron, his usually smooth forehead puckered in a frown.

'What is strange?' asked the Professor.

'Those two suns. When I was last here there was only one.'

'Are you sure of that?'

'How could I be mistaken? We remarked on it, because on some of the early pictures two suns were shown in the sky. I remember our guide pointing them out to us as if they had a particular meaning. Seeing only one sun we couldn't understand what he meant, and came to the conclusion that the two suns depicted had merely some symbolic significance. Which is why I did not mention this when I described the planet to you. Now it looks as if the pictures told the truth.'

'We must assume that one of the suns is not constant in its position,' said the Professor. 'Never mind. Let us go down.'

The *Tavona* was soon low enough for the surface of Selinda to be broadly surveyed. It was as Borron had described it, a pleasant world with luxuriant vegetation and some animals grazing on the open ground. There were also several towns. From high above these appeared to be no great distance apart, but Rex knew from experience that actually they were widely separated. The devastated area referred to by Borron was conspicuous. The centre was black, surrounding what appeared to be an enormous hole. Quantities of the black substance also lay around on the yellow sand, some at a considerable distance, as if it had been blown out of the hole.

Apparently Tiger noticed this, too, for he remarked quietly to Rex, who was at his elbow: 'That must be where the black building-material was obtained. It looks to me mighty like the crater of an extinct volcano.'

'When it was active it might have coughed up that black stuff,' suggested Rex.

'There's no doubt that's where it came from.'

The topic was not continued, for the Professor's interest was elsewhere. 'One would have expected to see roads', he observed.

'There were still traces of roads when I was here,' replied Borron. 'It seems they have become overgrown.'

'Not a hopeful sign of finding anyone alive.'

'I told you,' reminded Borron, 'the men we saw had given up doing anything. They had not even troubled to repair their homes, which were in a state of dilapidation, much less the roads, for which there was no longer any use. The men were merely living out their time – or rather, existing.'

'As one would expect in the circumstances,' returned the Professor.

'I see the spot where we landed,' went on Borron. He pointed. 'Over there. You can still see the small dwellings where the survivors had gathered, on the outskirts of that rather large town.'

Silence fell as, with the jet-brakes checking their fall, the ship went on down and under Borron's directions came to rest where his previous landing had been made.

Rex, gazed through his window while precautionary atmospheric tests were made. Looking towards the town he could see the larger buldings in the centre rising above what was evidently the residential quarters; which, of course, was quite normal. But nowhere did he see anyone resembling a human being. The only movement was provided by some animals, of a species unknown to him, grazing not far away.

The doors were opened and sweet fresh air poured in. One by one the exploring party stepped out, Tiger carrying his rifle, and the Professor his electronic 'counter'.

For perhaps a minute, as they gazed about them, no one spoke. Then Borron said softly: As I prophesied, we have come too late. The men must all be dead, or they would be here.'

'In that case we must be content with what they have left behind them,' answered the Professor dolefully. 'Let us start with these houses – or what is left of them.'

7 The world that died

The Professor led the way slowly towards the houses. There were twelve. They stood close together in a straight row, so it did not take long to look into each one in turn. Every one was identical, simple in design and empty except for a few pieces of plain furniture. Dust that had long been undisturbed covered everything, floors, tables and household chattels. All the houses were in a state of disrepair, some well on the way to collapse.

'I wouldn't call this a very good effort for a race having high artistic attainments,' remarked Tiger, looking at the buildings. 'One would have expected to find something more in accord with their unique ability.'

'These were probably nothing more than temporary accommodation for men working in the fields,' conjectured Borron. 'In any case I told you the people have ceased to have an interest in anything. Without a future what was there to strive for? Beauty? Pleasure? Praise? Durability? To a man about to die all these things lose their appeal. Here we only see the end of a story, one that began a long time ago, I think.'

'A question that occurs to me is this,' put in Tiger. 'What became of the last man left alive? I mean, where is his body? He couldn't bury himself. When he knew his time had come one would expect him to retire to his bed. In one of the houses we should have found his remains.'

'He may have become deranged, gone away and destroyed himself; either that, or having a horror of this particular spot, wandered away into the country to die by himself like a sick animal,' said the Professor, bleakly. 'Well, as we have seen all there is to see here I suggest we move on to the town, for whatever that has to offer. I am curious to see these superb pictures and we have no time to waste. Apart from our own urgency I have an uneasy feeling that this place is not as healthy as it appears to be. Until we know what slew the inhabitants of Selinda, while we remain here we stand in some risk of sharing their fate.'

Vargo agreed.

The short walk to the town would have been pleasant enough had it not been for the deathly silence, the way passing through what had once been gardens, now much overgrown and gone wild. But the utter absence of sound near buildings was so unnatural that it seemed to worry the eardrums. As Rex remarked, instinctively speaking in a low voice, near a town, by day or by night, there are always some sounds, even though they may be distant. Here there was no sound, near or far, except those they themselves were making as they followed what had once been a well-made road, but was now overgrown with a jungle of trees, some in blossom and some bearing luscious-looking fruit. Flowering shrubs and a variety of flowers had sometimes to be pushed aside to allow a passage through them. The sun struck hot from a sky of deep blue, and Rex would have sampled some of the fruit to quench his thirst had not the Professor advised him against it.

'One of these fruits, or all of them, should the planet have been contaminated, may have been responsible for what has happened here,' said the Professor, seriously. 'Wait. Presently we may be able to confirm that, or otherwise.'

They passed some of the animals, great beasts of a bovine character with thick, rough, hairy coats. Some were moulting in large tufts, as a camel sheds its coat at intervals. The creatures stared at them with big, lack-lustre eyes, grass and saliva hanging from their mouths, but they made no hostile move.

'I would say those animals were once domesticated,' remarked the Professor. 'They have no fear of men, as one would expect if they were really wild. I have a suspicion, too, that they are not entirely happy.'

'How is it they have survived when their owners have died?' questioned Tiger.

'Their unusually thick hair may have afforded them some protection against the peril that struck down the people—and most other creatures as well, supposing there were some here. Once dead they could not return. With the vegetation it would be different,' the Professor pointed out. 'Even if the planet was swept clean, seeds in the ground could reproduce the species after the killer had passed.'

Presently Rex stumbled, and looking down to see what had caught his toe, saw it was a crumbling human skeleton.

'We must expect that,' remarked the Professor, at Rex's ejaculation of horror.

As they walked on they saw others.

'Death must have struck these poor creatures faster than their friends could bury them,' observed the Professor in a melancholy voice.

If the silence in the rural district had been uncanny, in the town it was little short of frightening. At least, Rex found it so, as they passed between small but beautiful houses of what had been the residential area surrounding larger buildings which could be seen farther on. Exquisitely carved statues of white marble stood like ghosts in what had been the gardens. All were in a sad state of neglect, some the prey of moss and lichen, others clad in living garments of climbing plants such as forms of ivy and convolvulus, the vivid scarlet flowers of which only seemed to emphasize the atmosphere of tragedy. The whole party must have felt this, for the conversation, after becoming desultory, died away altogether as they pushed their way up the weed-grown street. Rex found himself glancing furtively at the empty windows of the houses, still half expecting to see eyes watching them.

'Dreadful – dreadful,' murmured the Professor at last. 'To stand in the presence of death is always moving, but here, before a dead world, I find myself quite overwhelmed. Little could the people who once lived here have imagined such a picture as this. But there, one could say the same of Ancient Greece and Rome, where only ruins mark their former greatness. I must say, Borron, that while I agree the architecture is fine and noble, the decorative detail, the carvings of which you spoke, fall short of my expectations.'

'They were not like this when I was here,' declared Borron. 'Something has happened to them. They are beginning to disintegrate.'

'The stone looks hard, so they shouldn't be doing that yet,' said Tiger. 'They look to me as if they'd been sprayed with acid, or some corrosive substance.'

When they reached the central square of the town, Borron pointed. 'There is the black building I told you about.'

'Let's look inside,' suggested the Professor, eagerly.

'I'd look at the pictures first, if I were you, in case we bump into something unpleasant and miss our chance,' advised Tiger, cautiously.

The Professor hesitated. 'Perhaps you are right,' he agreed.

'Look!' cried Rex, suddenly. 'Smoke.' He pointed.

High up, some distance away, conspicuous in the deep blue dome of heaven, was a circular cloud of pure white smoke, slowly rising. As, speechless, they stared at it in amazement, a second cloud appeared below it, also rising. Then came a third. It did not move with the lazy conséquence of bonfire smoke, but curled upwards in the still air as if impelled by an unseen force. Even as they watched, yet another cloud was puffed up, so that presently there was a string of them, each isolated, one above the other.

'What an extraordinary phenomenon,' murmured the Professor in a hushed voice. 'Can somebody be making smoke signals?'

'If anything is making signals it is the planet itself, telling us to get out,' asserted Tiger, grimly. 'I know where that's coming from. It's a volcano. I noticed it as we came down, but it wasn't smoking then.'

The Professor held out his wrist so that he could see his watch. 'As regular as clockwork,' he reported, after watching several more puffs. 'One every fifteen seconds. My friends, we are watching the heartbeats of a planet.'

'It looks to me more like a planet with a bad cough,' muttered Tiger. 'And it doesn't only cough smoke. I fancy that it coughs up, among other things, the black stuff these wretched people used for building. Without any wind to carry it away any heavy particles in that smoke will fall back on the ground.'

'Could that have anything to do with what has happened here?' asked Rex, anxiously.

'Possibly – possibly,' answered the Professor. 'Indirectly if not directly.'

'I don't like it,' asserted Tiger. 'I suggest we get back to the ship.'

'I don't see any immediate cause for alarm,' returned the Professor. "Not while the volcano confines its activities to coughing only smoke. Having come so far we must see these pictures. We may never have another opportunity. Have we much farther to go, Borron?'

'No, we are almost there.'

'Then let us continue. Lead the way.'

They strode on, more briskly now, and soon Borron turned into a long white marble building. There were no doors. As he crossed the pillared threshold, his feet raising a fine white powdery dust, a cry of dismay broke from his lips. The others, hurrying forward, saw what had caused it. The paintings that had once lined the walls had lost their colour, and as if that were not bad enough, were peeling off in strips and flakes.

The Professor sat on one of the marble benches that ran the length of the hall in front of the picture gallery. Said he, in a voice that revealed his bitter disappointment: 'If these paintings were made for posterity the people who did them were not very clever. They should have used pigments of more durable quality. What a pity. Dear me, what a pity. Well, there it is. We have, it seems, made a fruitless journey.'

'It was not the fault of the artists, I am sure, that their work should so soon fall into decay,' said Borron. 'They must have been an ancient race, and as such would know from experience the lasting qualities of their materials. I would say that the same insidious invader that destroyed the people is now fast destroying their handiwork.' As Borron spoke his eyes were travelling along the line of pictures to the far end of the hall. 'Wait!' he exclaimed suddenly. 'What have we here?' He strode along the line behind the benches, to the final picture, and there he stopped, staring.

The others, who had followed him, needed no further explanation. There before them was a perfect picture.

'This has been done since I came here,' declared Borron. 'I am sure of it. I could not have forgotten such a picture.'

It showed a man, one man alone, standing on a heap of broken ruins. All around were more ruins. The man, white-haired and bearded, was looking up at the blue sky with his arms raised as if in supplication.

'That, I fancy, is the end of the story,' said the Professor, huskily, obviously very much moved. 'Gentlemen, we are looking at the portrait of the last survivor of the planet Selinda.'

It so happened that Tiger had chosen to walk down the aisle between the benches and the wall. Looking at something on the ground he said: 'And here is all that is left of him. A little while ago we wondered what had happened to the last man. Now we know. This is where he came, to paint the last word of the tragedy that we see around us.'

The others stepped forward to look. There, on the ground in a composed position, was the painter, his paints and brushes beside him. The body was very much decomposed, but not unpleasantly so. It appeared merely to have crumbled away, as had the carvings outside.

'One begins to wonder how many other peoples have vanished in this way,' said the Professor, quietly. 'Here, soon there will be nothing to show one existed. But let us not dwell on such morbid thoughts. Let us see if we can discover what played this awful havoc.'

He unslung the case that hung from his shoulder and took out the instrument it contained. One glance told them all they needed to know. The needle was swinging wildly. They could hear it ticking.

'I was right!' cried the Professor. 'The whole place must be alive with radioactivity. We must go at once, or we, too, may become infected.'

No one argued about this decision and the party retired with some haste to the street. Even there the instrument was still giving positive results. Passing the black building on their way out of the town it reacted with alarming violence.

'We need not go in,' said the Professor, hurrying on. 'We know what we wanted to know. That place must be a death trap, the more perilous because the danger cannot be seen.'

They stopped only once on their way back to the ship, and then it was to allow the Professor to test the fruit Rex would have eaten on the way to the town.

'A good thing you didn't put that into your inside, my boy,' was all the Professor had to say about it. But it was enough.

They wasted no time when they reached the *Tavona*.

'Away! Away!' cried the Professor. 'The place is evil, and every moment we stay here adds to the risk of infection, not only of ourselves but of the ship.'

The *Tavona* hurtled away into space, leaving a little cloud of dust to mark the spot where it had stood.

'Well, Professor, and what do you make of all that?' asked Tiger, when they were well clear.

The Professor smiled wanly. 'My opinion, for what it is worth, is this. The people of Selinda, taken up as they were with art, knew nothing of science. That is understandable. The two things seldom go together. There may have been a fall-out of radiation from the sky; something to do with that wandering sun, perhaps. But I think it more likely the trouble started when they found, and exploited for building and carving, that black rock which without question was highly radioactive. They were not to know its deadly nature. They knew something was happening to them but could not guess what it was. Everyone and everything became infected, the first to go, no doubt, being the people who handled the stuff and, for what reason I wouldn't hazard a guess, the women. The men would, of course take the contamination into their homes. Eventually, without having the least idea of what was killing them, they associated death with the black rock. Some of the people fled; but it was too late. They had already been affected and took the slow death with them. Thus, the whole planet became involved in the disaster.'

'Do you think this contamination will persist?' asked Rex.

'I couldn't answer that,' admitted the Professor. 'It may die out in time. If it doesn't, there is a chance that the emanations of Selinda may affect neighbouring planets.'

'Thank goodness Earth isn't one of them,' said Tiger.

'There may already be more man-made radioactivity there now than is good for us,' said the Professor, seriously.

The *Tavona* raced on, on its way back to Petroconda.

8 On to Terromagna

The return trip to Petroconda was a rather dismal affair, for the fate of the unlucky people of Selinda weighed heavily upon them all, if for no other reason than that it showed with graphic clarity how a world could be snuffed out as easily as a candle-flame by the mighty forces of the Universe which, once released, were beyond human control.

However, the voyage to Petroconda was made without mishap, and it was with relief that Rex saw Toby, and the ship that had taken him to Mino, standing beside the marker pyramid.

They would now, he thought, go home. Feeling depressed he hoped so. Home meant the planet Earth. It was strange, he brooded, that he should still think of Earth as a safe retreat, a place of refuge, although in his heart he realized that it must be just as vulnerable to extinction as any other world. Yet the people there were rushing about their tasks and pleasures, most of them blissfully unaware of what was happening in the skies around them, unmindful of the fact that the ball of soil and water on which they were standing was also rushing about at the whim of the almighty forces that really governed the Universe. They were, he thought, like a lot of ants on a piece of driftwood, racing along on a river in spate towards an ocean without shores where they would one day, maybe tomorrow or a million years hence, disappear without trace. One ripple on the way would be enough to overturn them.

Such morbid reflections were banished when the *Tavona* touched down, and in a few moments the reunion had been made.

'You found the message we left for you?' the Professor asked Toby.

'Yes. How did you get on? Anything exciting?'

'It was exciting up to a point, but it was also a bit depressing,' answered Tiger. 'There's nobody left alive on Selinda and at the rate the place is falling to pieces it won't be long before nothing will be there to show that it was once occupied by what must have been a fine race of people.'

'What caused the mischief?'

'The Professor thinks radiation, or something like it. Everything seems to be saturated with it, but where it came from is still a question. A volcano came to life while we were there so we lost no time getting away.'

'Never mind Selinda; we can talk of that later,' came in the Professor. 'Let us have your news. Did you bring the spade?'

'Yes, and we have used it.'

'You mean you've buried the dead men?'

'While we were waiting for you.'

'Good. I was dreading the task. No more storms?'

'Not while we've been here.'

'How is Quantos?'

'Oh, he's pretty well back to normal except for his ankle. Apart from that there wasn't much the matter with him. I waited for a little while on Mino hoping to get some definite news of Ardilla, but none worth speaking of has come in. Rolto isn't back yet, nor any of the others who went scouting. The only ship that came in was from Terromagna, to ask if Multavo was all right. I gather it had to go half-way round the Universe to get to Mino without falling foul of Ardilla – and that route won't be open much longer.'

'Didn't the Terromagna ship bring news?' asked Multavo.

'No good news. According to the scientists on Terromagna, what it was thought might happen is now happening. Ardilla is projecting its rays, or beams, still farther, so that its influence is greater than ever.'

'What I would like to know is the form these rays or beams take,' said the Professor. 'That is to say, are these projections literally beams, on a single wavelength, or do they fill the entire atmosphere? In the latter case it would be impossible to escape them.'

'How did the Terromagna ship manage to get through?' asked Multavo.

Toby answered. 'The position as I understand it is this. In the Third Region, between Mino and Terromagna there are some suns, two of them tremendous. The orbit of Ardilla lies roughly midway between them, which means that its rays, operating in all directions, form a barrier through which no ship can pass without being affected. To outflank these rays, assuming there is a limit to their range, would mean passing so close to one sun or the other that a ship attempting it would be scorched, if not burnt up. At present the trip is still possible because that is how the Terromagna ship got through; but from all accounts it was touch and go. The heat in the ship, as it passed dangerously near the sun, nearly cooked the crew. Should the range of these rays be extended even that route would be closed.'

'One would either have to risk the rays or be roasted by one sun or the other.'

'Exactly. That is how the captain of the Terromagna ship put it to me.'

'Where is this ship now?' Multavo asked Toby.

'On Mino. The Captain is waiting to discuss the matter with you. He thinks that by making a tremendous detour you might get through; but if you fail, if the rays reach you, you've had it; or words to that effect.'

'In that case I'd better get along.'

'There doesn't seem much to discuss,' put in Vargo. 'If Ardilla has closed that section of space to shipping nothing can be done about it.'

'Something will have to be done about it,' declared the Professor. 'If Ardilla goes on extending its zone of influence, and we may suppose it will, it can only be a matter of time before it controls the entire Universe. The survival of everyone, everywhere, will therefore depend on Ardilla being put out of action.'

'How are you going to set about Ardilla?' questioned Tiger, sceptically.

'I have no idea,' confessed the Professor. 'But it will have to be done somehow. Tell me, Doctor, what effect did these rays have on the Terromagna ship, if any?'

'The crew was aware of a feeling of paralysis and had increasing difficulty in keeping control not only of their limbs but of their brains. That, they admit, might have been due in some degree to the awful heat in the ship. There seems to be more than one type of ray.'

The Professor polished his spectacles.

'Are you contemplating a declaration of war against Ardilla?' Tiger asked him.

'If by that you mean invading the planet, my dear fellow, the answer is no. That is obviously out of the question for the simple reason that it is impossible to get near the place. Ardilla will have to be subdued by its own weapons.'

'You mean, by rays?' Multavo put the question.

'Yes. If Ardilla can produce rays of such force it should be possible for scientists on Terromagna, who seem to be well informed on the subject, to do the same thing. Alternatively, they will have to build a ship that is in some way insulated against all rays. It should be possible. Every new weapon on Earth has produced a counter-weapon.'

Tiger stepped in again. 'Another alternative would be to split the rays or change their direction.' He smiled at Vargo's expression. 'Even we backward people on Earth could do that,' he affirmed. 'In the last great war our enemies put out rays to guide their aircraft. We bent them, so that the aircraft went off their course and unloaded their bombs far from the objective.'

'It might even be possible,' said the Professor, thoughtfully, 'to cause the rays to recoil on the stations discharging them. Anyhow, Ardilla must be taught a lesson and we shall find a way to do it.'

'We shan't solve the problem standing here,' stated Tiger. 'It looks to me as if, in the interests of everyone, the matter should be the subject of an interplanetary conference. Even so, sooner or later someone will have to take the risk of finding out the purpose of these rays, what effect they have and the limit of their range.'

'That is true,' murmured Vargo.

'I think for a start I had better get back to Mino and discuss with my friends there the possibility of returning to Terromagna,' decided Multavo.

'In that case I suggest we move off before another storm comes along to make things uncomfortable,' said Tiger.

This was agreed. Toby rejoined his own party in the *Tavona*, and in a few minutes both ships were on their way back to Mino.

No trouble was encountered *en route* and in due course, they landed on their home base to find matters still as Toby had described them. The Professor went off with Vargo to discuss the situation with the High Council while Multavo went over to talk with the captain of the Terromagna ship. Leaving his father and Toby to overhaul their kit, Rex departed with Morino to relax with his feet on good solid ground.

In this way two days passed pleasantly enough: then the conferences came to an end without any definite decision having been made except that Multavo declared his intention of trying to get back to Terromagna by a new long-distance route. Vargo had volunteered, and had been given permission, to reconnoitre the direction taken by Rolto to see if contact could be made with him. There were a number of planets in the region and it was thought he might be on one of them, possibly having trouble with his ship.

After Multavo had departed Vargo told the Professor that he and his party would be well advised to remain on Mino; or, if they wished, Gator would take them back to Earth; but the Professor would not hear of it. The Ardilla problem, he claimed, would ultimately affect Earth, and the least he could do was keep in touch with events.

After some argument it was agreed – as Rex had expected all along – that the Earth party should go with the *Tavona* on its quest for information, perhaps, at a later date, to meet Multavo again on Terromagna should both ships manage to get through. On Terromagna, they knew from their conversations with Multavo, there were wonders they had not yet seen.

'This is going to be a long journey,' warned Borron who, as navigator, was plotting the course while preparations were being made.

'You are hoping to keep clear of anything Ardilla might do?' queried the Professor.

'Yes, of course.'

'If you do that we shall learn nothing new about it.'

'If we venture within range of the rays we are less likely to learn anything,' put in Tiger, meaningly.

'Let me make the position clear,' interposed Vargo. 'The intention in the first instance is to make a wide detour with Terromagna as the ultimate objective. We shall follow the course Rolto said he would take, calling at planets *en route* for news of him. Our real difficulty lies in the fact that we do not know the extreme range of the Ardilla rays, although we can assume that with distance they will lose some of their force. But they may have reached Dacoona. It would not surprise me if we found Multavo there, should he have escaped the rays, because he said he intended to make another visit to collect the scientists who are willing to have their special glands examined. But that is by the way. I hope by calling at different planets, with orbits at varying distances from Ardilla, to establish how far the influence of Ardilla has already penetrated.'

'Very well,' answered the Professor. 'The venture is your responsibility so we can only put ourselves in your hands. You must do whatever you think best and with that we shall abide. We understand the risks and are prepared to accept them.'

'Good,' acknowledged Vargo. 'Then let us proceed.'

9 More problems

The *Tavona* was soon on its difficult and dangerous mission. No trouble was expected in the early stages of the flight, but as it drew nearer to the region where the potent forces of Ardilla were probing ever farther into space the travellers became increasingly alert for the first indication of the peril.

They called at several minor planets, some of them inhabited, but only a few by species that could be described as human and fewer still by types that could be called intelligent. But, as the Professor remarked, it was interesting to be able to observe, even from a distance, humanity in its various degrees of development, eras through which, as Rex was aware, the human species on Earth had passed to reach its present civilization; a civilization now so complicated, the Professor had often declared, that it was a question how much farther it could go without collapsing in a state of chaos.

They neither saw nor heard anything of Rolto, although their method of conducting a search was inevitably somewhat haphazard. Apart from using their eyes all they could do was circumnavigate each planet as they came to it, circling and quartering slowly at a low altitude calling on the radio. On the rare occasions where Gator or Borron knew there was an atmosphere, and the people were to be trusted, a landing was made and questions were asked. Actually, this was done, as much as for any other reason, to provide an opportunity for refreshment and exercise as a break from the monotony of space travel, all the more tedious because the ship was travelling at a velocity much lower than usual.

There were, Vargo had explained, several reasons for this

comparatively slow progress. Firstly, they were in no hurry. Secondly, they would be more likely to strike a period in each constellation when Rolto might be making signals. And last, but not least, by travelling slowly they would feel the first effects of Ardilla's rays, should they encounter them, and thus have an opportunity to retire before they were badly affected. At the maximum velocity they would hurtle into them and perhaps succumb before they could take evasive action.

Actually, the wily old navigator, Borron, was bearing other possibilities in mind, as he mentioned later in the course of conversation. They were now approaching one of the great suns of the Third Region galaxy. How far its heat extended was not known, but it would certainly be an astronomical distance. At maximum velocity they might plunge into the furnace and become incandescent, a minute shooting star, before they could withdraw. In point of fact, as they were all aware, this could happen should they plunge too quickly into any atmosphere; but it was a routine rule of space travel never to approach at high speed any planet of a size that would indicate a dense or far-reaching envelope of air, irrespective of what such an atmosphere might consist. And they were, after all, in a region that had not been fully explored.

As Rex was now able to appreciate, there was so much to explore that it seemed unlikely there could ever be an end to space exploration. On Earth, he pondered, it had taken men a long time to explore their own little world. And while the *Tavona's* crew were all men of great experience they could no more say they had been everywhere than a sailor at home could claim to have set foot on every island in the Seven Seas.

Accustomed as he was by now to space travel it never failed to give Rex a shock when he realized what he was doing: moving from world to world with less effort than would be involved in travelling from country to country on his home planet. Here, in space, there were no booking offices, no changing from road to rail and from rail to ship. No tickets, no passports.

Yet such a voyage as the one on which they were engaged could hardly pass without adventure, and he was turning over in his mind this very subject, the absence of anything like formalties at their ports of call, when he saw a discussion going on between Vargo, Gator and Borron, apparently, from the way they were looking at it, about a body that had appeared ahead on their line of flight. It was obviously not a star, burning with its own fires; it was too dim for that. It could only be a planet, or large planetoid, how large it was as yet impossible to say. Borron consulted his chart.

It turned out, as a result of a question put by the Professor, that no one had ever seen this planet before. It was not shown on Borron's chart. However, the old navigator was neither surprised nor perturbed. He had known the same sort of thing to happen more than once. The planet, he thought, was either a newcomer to the region or one with an orbit so tremendous that it had been away for a long time.

'In that case we're not likely to find anything alive on it,' said Tiger.

'That doesn't necessarily follow,' answered the Professor. 'Provided the planet did not meet with serious trouble on its journey any people who might be on it may be as unaware of their travels as are most of the people on Earth. How many of our friends at home realize that every day their little world, and the Solar System of which it is a unit, has changed its position in space a matter of half a million miles? I suggest we have a close look at this stranger since it is on our course.'

'The same idea may have occurred to Rolto, who was coming this way,' said Vargo. 'Apart from his own peculiar views, Rolto is a fine navigator and a keen explorer, so should he have seen this new arrival in the region it is more than likely he would stop to have a look at it. We might do the same in the hope of finding him, or some trace of him, there. What do you think, Gator?'

Gator was looking hard at the planet. 'It is not a place of any great size, but from its colour I would say it has an atmosphere,' replied the *Tavona's* commander. 'I can also tell you this. Being so far from any sun it will be cold, and as the only light it can receive will be reflected light from other planets we must be prepared to find it – what is your word? – gloomy.'

They all stood at their windows to watch the unknown planet, already the size of a large moon, shining faintly with reflected light. The jet-brakes came on when the slowly changing colour of the sky around them, from almost black to deep blue, told them that Gator's opinion about an atmosphere was correct. Radio signals calling Rolto were broadcast but there was no reply.

To Rex, as usual, came the apprehensive thrill of venturing into the unknown. What, he wondered, were they soon to see? He had, or thought he had, learned to be prepared for anything. But he thought that before, and in almost every case he had been wrong. Events had far outstripped imagination.

As they dropped still nearer he derived some comfort from what features could be seen on the surface of this wanderer in space, for they were not unlike those of Earth, approached in a temperate zone in winter. He could make out mountains, plains, deserts, seas and rivers. There were large areas of forest, too, some of sombre hue, as if they might be conifers; others, dead or deciduous, had shed their leaves. Altogether it looked a drab, dreary place. They looked in vain for signs of human occupation, such as towns and road connecting them, usually visible from a high altitude. Still, observation was not easy, for in the absence of sunlight there were of course no shadows. There was not even a satellite moon to help matters, so that everything was the same grey, colour-less half-tone.

'There's no one here,' remarked Tiger, confidently.

'One can never be sure until one has landed,' asserted Vargo. 'One could approach Earth from some directions without seeing signs of life.'

'But without a sun how could there be life?' put in the Professor, 'Sunlight and the warmth it provides is the source of life.'

'Do not forget that conditions here may not always be the same as we see them now,' reminded Borron. 'Should this planet have, as I believe, an exceptionally long orbit, it might, on its journey, come within the influence of not one sun but several.'

'That would result in periodical changes of temperature, with resultant effects on everything on it.'

'Of course. But we have no idea of how long each succes-sive phase might last. It might be a million years, or more. Nor have we any means at this moment of judging whether the planet is on its way to utter darkness, with extreme cold, or a more temperate zone.'

'Even so, it seems unlikely that any form of intelligent life could endure such diverse conditions,' argued the Professor. 'Every time the planet entered a region of extreme cold, as we see it now, all warm-blooded creatures would die.'

'Should the abnormal phases be regular, intelligent crea-tures might adapt themselves to them. You yourself have said that intelligent life can adapt itself to any conditions, pro-vided the changes do not occur too quickly. On Earth, you have told me, you have people living happily in the Arctic Circle, while others have chosen for their place of abode the burning heat of the desert. Both types survive.'

'But they could not change places.'

'There is, I assume, no need for them to do so. Had that become imperative they would, given unlimited time, have found a means to ensure their survival.'

While this conversation was going on Gator had taken the ship down to an altitude of perhaps a thousand feet; but still no movement could be seen. Moving horizontally the ship now made wide circuits, covering each hemisphere in turn. It looked the same everywhere, dim, grey and apparently lifeless.

'If Rolto is here he's a dead man,' declared Tiger. 'Vargo, do you still believe it is possible for life to exist on such a depressing place as this?'

'To that I can only answer, I don't know,' replied Vargo. 'I have only said it is not impossible for some form of life to be here, for if my travels have taught me one thing it is that in the Universe nothing is impossible. Once you have grasped that you will cease to be astonished by anything you see. You, who are new to interplantary exploration, in spite of yourselves still make the fundamental mistake of judging all things by what applies on Earth, where, as with every unit in the Universe, large or small, conditions are as that particular environment has made them. For an example, of all the people who live on Earth no two are absolutely identical, in appearance or mental capacity. Thus it is with worlds.'

'I am beginning to realize that must be so, but when confronted by what appears to be quite preposterous one finds it hard to accept,' returned the Professor, somewhat lamely. 'More than once I have hesitated to trust my eyes.'

'You'll get over that in time,' said Borron, cheerfully.

'Are you going to land?' the Professor asked Gator.

'I will if you wish, although there doesn't seem to be much point in it. Rolto would not have landed here except in desperate emergency. I have warned you, you will find it very cold.'

'We do not stay long. The place can go down in my records for what it is.'

'Say, rather for what it appears to be,' replied Vargo,

vaguely. 'In space exploration what a place is, and what it appears to be, are not always the same thing.'

'Let's go down and settle the argument,' requested Toby, impatiently.

'Try that open space in the arid region,' suggested the Professor, 'But just a minute. There seems to be something there although I can't see exactly what it is. This miserable twilight is most deceptive.'

'It looks to me like a super molehill,' said Tiger.

'With a hole in the side, at the base,' observed Rex.

The ship went on down and presently came to rest on a flat, gravel surface, near what Tiger had called a molehill, and was in fact a gigantic, conical-shaped heap of earth.

'If that was made by a mole it must be some mole,' joked Toby.

'One thing is quite certain; that heap is artificial,' asserted the Professor, while the usual atmospheric tests were made. 'It was thrown up by somebody or something. At least, I can think of no natural upheaval that could have caused it. Its regular shape rules that out. Let us go and have a look at it. I have never seen anything like it before.'

Neither had Rex seen anything quite like it, although the hole, some six or eight feet across, and as high, might have been the entrance to a railway tunnel had the floor not sloped steeply down into the ground. In the weird half-light the enormous pile of soil, so perfect in shape, had the makings of a first-class mystery.

'What beats me is where an artificial mountain, enough soil and rock to make an artificial mountain, came from,' he remarked. 'It couldn't have come from outside.'

'In which case it must have come from inside, my boy,' returned the Professor.

'But what labour!'

'As you say, what labour. An army must have been needed to make it.'

'I know this,' put in Toby. 'It must be jolly cold outside. It's chilly even in here.'

'That was to be expected, without a sun,' said Vargo. 'You can go out if you wish. There is enough atmosphere to make spacesuits unnecessary. That also was as we expected.'

'Why?' asked Rex.

'Because intelligent creatures, able to build a thing like this, would almost certainly need air. Of course, they may no longer be here, but we shall have to be careful. Anything could be inside that mound.'

'Let's see what it is,' said the Professor, moving to the doors.

'Don't go far or you may be overcome by cold,' warned Vargo, as he opened the doors, to let in a flood of air so cold that it nearly took Rex's breath away.

Tiger picked up his rifle. 'We may need it, you never know,' he remarked, as the Professor looked at him questioningly.

'If the men who made this fantastic monument are still here, and decide to attack us, I doubt if bullets would stop them,' murmured the Professor.

'I wasn't thinking of men.'

'What were you thinking of?'

Tiger shrugged. 'I haven't a clue.'

'Then let's find one,' suggested Toby.

10 Land of twilight

The Professor, agog with his usual interest for anything new, was first out of the ship, his breath showing like smoke in the chill air. Followed by Rex, Tiger, Toby and Vargo, he strode briskly over the short distance that separated the ship from the entrance to the mound, which could now be seen, without any doubt whatever, to be an artificial and not a natural formation. A certain amount of rough dry-walling round the mouth of the hole, to support the roof, settled that. Inside, the floor sloped more steeply downwards than Rex had supposed, looking at it from the ship.

As the Professor walked on, with his usual disregard for danger, to examine the hole more closely, a litle cry of surprise left his lips.

'What is it?' asked Tiger, following quickly, rifle at the ready.

'Come here!'

They all joined the Professor.

'Why, it's warm!' exclaimed Rex, in a voice stiff with surprise.

The temperature at the mouth of the hole was several degrees higher than elsewhere. They went right up to the hole and stared at it. The dim light prevented them from seeing more than a few yards inside what now appeared to be a black tunnel. It was not imagination. Here the atmosphere was warm and humid. Moreover it had a sour, musty smell.

'There's somebody, or something, in there,' declared Tiger.

'It isn't a human smell,' murmured the Professor, looking puzzled.

'And it isn't like any animal smell I've ever encountered – the sort of smell you get at zoos.'

For a moment, they stood silent. Then the Professor took another pace forward. 'Listen,' he said.

The others complied, but the hole might have been a tomb for all the sound that came from it.

'Well, Vargo: you're a man of experience. What do you make of it?' inquired the Professor.

Vargo lifted a shoulder. 'I have never seen anything like this,' was all he could say.

'If there are people in there they must be asleep,' averred Tiger.

'Or so far away that any sounds they might make can't reach us,' put in Rex.

'No, that won't do,' rejoined the Professor. 'What about ventilation? You can't live in a tunnel of any length without a through draught, or a constant supply of fresh air. What do you say, Tiger? You're the engineer of the party.'

'In my opinion this isn't an entrance, as we naturally supposed. It's an exit, The warm air is coming out of this hole, so it follows that air is going in somewhere. From the absence of footprints on the ground the place doesn't appear to have been used lately, although, of course, in sand and gravel footprints wouldn't last very long.'

'We are agreed that there is something here – something alive.'

'Definitely. The stink proves that.'

'But what about the heat? Where does that come from?' asked Rex. 'Could it come from deep down in the ground?'

'It might,' agreed his father. 'But don't forget that a lot of people huddled in a confined space can themselves raise a temperature almost to body heat.'

'All right. There are people in here,' said Rex. 'What do they do for light?'

'It is a provision of nature that nocturnal creatures are able to see in the dark,' reminded the Professor. 'Anything living on a sunless planet would almost certainly develop that faculty.'

'What about food?'

'Wild creatures with us at home either eat much in pre-paration for winter or they store food against such time when none is available. I see nothing about that could be used as food, and as the creatures that live here, whatever they may be, must be warm-blooded, we may assume, I think, that they would have the sense to do that. If, as we believe, this planet has an exceptionally large orbit, in which it passes through extremes of temperature, anything on it would know that and take steps to preserve its life during the period of cold.'

'Well, what are we going to do about it?' asked Tiger. 'If we stand here much longer in this stink I shall be sick. If we get out of it we're likely to get frost-bitten.'

'Let us investigate farther,' said the Professor, brightly. 'This is a problem that must be solved.'

'Be careful,' warned Vargo, seriously.

'I was thinking of going only a little way in,' replied the Professor. 'Fetch the torches, Rex.'

Rex hurried through the cold air between the cave and the ship, and having told Gator what was intended took two torches from their kit back to where the others were waiting.

His father was saying: 'I suggest that before we take on something we know nothing about we should test my theory by looking for the other end of this outsized fox hole. I'm sure there must be one. We may find a clue there as to what this is all about.'

'We would freeze in this icy atmosphere,' said Vargo, who was already shivering, having removed himself from the unpleasant aroma.

'I wasn't thinking of walking,' answered Tiger. 'This tunnel may run for miles. We'd cover the ground faster in the ship. If the other end is anything like this, and we may suppose it is, we could hardly miss it.'

'I think that is a sound idea,' said the Professor. 'I don't think I could face this abominable stench, which would, I suspect, become worse if we made an entrance at this end. It should be less objectionable at the intake.'

This was agreed and they all returned to the ship. Doors were closed against the cold and the search began, Gator taking the *Tavona* slowly over the ground at a height of about a hundred feet. Again they looked in vain for any sign of life, but there was not a movement anywhere. There was no wind, so even the trees stood stiff and stark in the cold grey light. Rex had never seen a landscape so desolate.

'What a place to be born in,' muttered Tiger, disgustedly. 'People at home who complain about our weather should have a look at this No wonder the inhabitants go underground to get out of it.'

It was Rex who spotted the mound at the far end of the tunnel. It was identical with the exit, the same enormous heap of soil and a gaping mouth even larger. It occurred on rising ground – in fact, on a plateau.

'We shan't find warm air here,' declared Tiger.

'Why not?' asked Rex. 'This end is higher than the other. Warm air rises.'

'And cold air falls. I fancy I can see how the tunnel is ventilated. The hole at this end is larger than the other. The cold air falls in, and under its pressure the air which has been warmed *en route* is pushed out at the far end. Anyway, that's how it looks to me. What do you say, Professor?'

'A primitive device, as one would expect, but possible. It implies that whoever or whatever lives here is endowed with sufficient intelligence to work that out. To my mind there is no doubt whatever that what we see is a place of retreat in inclement weather.'

'It seems queer that the people don't come out,' said Rex.

'Why should they? Can you see anything to come out for?'

'No.'

'That's the answer. They stay below to keep warm.'

'What a life! How long do you suppose they stay there?'

The Professor answered, 'Until the planet warms up on its approach to a sun. How long that may take we don't know, and never shall know unless Borron is clever enough to work out the orbit.'

'What could the people do while they're down in the ground?'

'Sleep, probably. We might ask what certain creatures do on Earth while they spend the winter in holes, in the ground, in trees, or in anything that happens to be available. Everything makes provision for its survival. It must, or it will die. Some store food against the time when none is to be had. Some of the things they do are quite incredible. Bees, with their combs of honey, provide a good example.'

'What sort of creatures would you expect to find here?'

'That, my boy, is a question impossible to answer – unless we go down the tunnel to find out.'

'Are you contemplating doing that?'

'Why not?'

'If you go down that hole it is unlikely that you will ever come out,' said Vargo, seriously. 'Whatever the creatures may be that live there they would not welcome an invader – unless, of course, he provided them with a little extra food.'

By this time the ship had landed near the entrance, and the same party as before walked forward to peer into it. Tiger's theory was soon proved to be correct, for here there was no smell and no heat. On the contrary, a slight draught of cold air was perceptible.

'If you take my advice,' said Vargo to the Professor, 'you will not interfere. Let us go before we are discovered. Already a scout may be watching us from inside.'

'Don't ask me to go leaving unsolved the most fascinating mystery we have encountered on this trip,' protested the

Professor. 'Such is my devouring curiosity that I simply must know what did this.'

'Your curiosity will be the death of you.'

'I expected you to say that, my dear fellow. You have said it before. My answer to that is, if curiosity is not the death of me something else will be, so what does it matter? An explorer without curiosity would serve no useful purpose. The rest of you can wait here, or, if you prefer, retire to the ship. You may be sure I shall do my best to return, but should I fail to do so the fault will be entirely my own.'

'I'll come with you,' offered Rex, recklessly.

'No, no,' disputed the Professor. 'There is no reason why my curiosity should be the death of *you*.'

'Well, make up your minds,' requested Vargo, a trifle impatiently. 'The ship will become cold, and the crew uncomfortable, while we are standing here.'

'Give me one of those torches, Rex,' ordered the Professor.

Rex handed one to him, and with it in his hand the Professor strode purposefully into the black depths that yawned before them.

'I'm not going to be left standing here,' decided Tiger. He hitched his rifle forward and followed.

Rex and Toby, after a glance at each other, walked on behind him.

They went on for some distance, slowly, always descending, in dead silence, the two torches cutting white wedges in a darkness that was now absolute. Progress was simplified by the tunnel being straight, so that it was possible to see some way ahead. Nothing happened. Once Rex took a furtive glance over his shoulder at the rapidly diminishing circle of grey light that marked the exit to the outside world and only with difficulty suppressed a desire to rush back to it, for he found the awful silence a greater strain on the nerves than had there been noises, however menacing.

Bracing himself to be prepared for something to happen

at any moment he kept on with the others, the floor always going downhill. The air was cold, although not as bitingly cold as it was outside, and reasonably fresh, although more than once he caught a whiff of the nauseating smell that had been so noticeable at the far end of the tunnel.

A little later the Professor stopped, held up his head and sniffed.

'I smell formic acid,' he said softly. 'I fancy we are in nothing more exciting than an ants' nest.'

'I hope you're right,' answered Tiger. 'As long as the ants are not of a size comparable with the hole they've made,' he added.

Rex hoped they would now go back, but far from that the Professor continued on with more assurance.

Presently he stopped again. So did they all, as from some distance ahead came a curious clicking noise, a sort of rattle, as if a can with small stones in it had been shaken.

'What do you suppose that was?' whispered the Professor.

'I haven't a clue,' replied Tiger. 'But it tells us that someone is at home. All I can say is, if that noise was made by an ant it must be a whopper.'

'I think we must be getting near the nest,' returned the Professor.

'And I think that one of the occupants has heard us.'

The light of Rex's roving torch was reflected suddenly by two round objects the size of tea plates. They were red, and glowed like hot coals. There could, Rex knew, be only one explanation. The objects were eyes. His stomach seemed to drop into his shoes.

Again came the rattle, louder than before, as if a man in armour had shaken himself. It was repeated several times in the distance. Points of light appeared beyond the first.

'Let's get out of this,' said Tiger, crisply. 'It looks as if we've started something.'

'I think you're right,' agreed the Professor, beginning to

walk backwards. 'Let us go quickly. I see no reason to panic. They may not follow us. They are probably as surprised as we are.'

Rex hoped sincerely that they would not be followed, for it was already clear to him that the creatures of the cave were not the sort with which to become involved; certainly not in the darkness of the cave. He, too, began to walk backwards, with alacrity, for his torch, still focused on the eyes, was also picking out faint gleams on the body of the thing, as if shining on a dark-coloured, highly polished shell. Moreover, the glints were becoming brighter, suggesting that the creature was advancing.

The rattle was now loud and incessant, filling the air with such a clatter as might have been made by an iron-clad army on the march. A suffocating, acrid smell swept up the cave.

In spite of the Professor's demand that there should be no panic the retreat soon became a rout; and once within striking distance of the exit everyone abandoned pretence and fled! With safety, or what was presumed to be safety, in sight, Tiger spun round and fired three shots in quick succession into the darkness behind. In the confined space the reports were deafening, but even so they failed to drown the clamour they produced. To Rex it sounded like a hundred dustbins rolling down a flight of stone steps.

Reaching the gloomy outside world they did not stop but raced on to the ship, Vargo shouting something in his own language to Borron who was standing between the doors, watching.

They literally fell into the ship. Rex was first on his feet, and dashing to a window to see what was happening outside was horrified to see such a mob pouring out of the cave that his eyes saucered with fear and amazement.

The creatures *were* ants. Or something like ants. But not the sort of ants one could crush underfoot. They were black, shining as if they had been polished, and about three feet tall as they ran in an erect position. The bodies were in two parts, joined in the middle by a ridiculously small waist. The upper part seemed to be all head, equipped with two great bulging eyes and jaws that never stopped snapping. They came on without pause, crowding and pushing each other as they rushed at the ship. Not a few, but hundreds. More were coming out. The entrance to the cave was packed with them. The numbers seemed to be endless as they continued to pour out in a furious flood.

Rex shuddered, for although the creatures were undoubtedly ants of a sort there was something horribly human about their deliberate actions, particularly about the way they used their arms, or forelegs – it was not clear which.

By now the others were at their windows, watching. Any danger appeared to have passed, for Gator had the ship on the move before the ant-men could reach it. At the height of a few feet, however, he stopped at the Professor's request so that they could have a close view of what was happening below. The Professor grabbed his camera to take a photograph, and went to the doors for that purpose.

'Watch out!' yelled Tiger, suddenly. 'They can fly!'

This was obviously true, for the leading files of ants had unfolded unsuspected wings, coarse but transparent, and were still in pursuit.

As Gator shot the ship up to a really safe height the Professor exclaimed: 'Dear me! That's better. We don't want any of those in the ship with us. I was right about the occupants being ants.'

'You didn't say what sort of ants,' growled Tiger.

'How was I to know? My eyes are still smarting from the beastly formic acid they exude. You were certainly right, my dear fellow, when you remarked that we had started something. Really, you know, once we had caught the faint smell of formic acid, and realized we were in the home of a species of ant, we should not have been surprised by what we saw, or by what happened. The only abnormal thing about these particular ants is their size, and for that the dimensions of the tunnel should have prepared us. In other respects the creatures behaved much as they do at home, where, you may or may not know, there are about two thousand species.'

'But these monsters were engineers, which means they were able to think,' declared Tiger.

'That could be argued, and is in fact argued by some naturalists, for our own ants, which, fortunately remain small. Should they ever achieve the size of these specimens they would overrun the Earth and make themselves masters of it. That, I suspect, has happened here.'

'I know our ants live in colonies, where strict discipline is maintained,' put in Rex.

'That is not all,' resumed the Professor. 'Some build mounds six or seven feet high. They keep their homes clean by removing all unwanted objects. They store food and, like us, eat both vegetable and animal matter.'

'Which means they would have eaten us, had they caught us.'

'Without the slightest doubt. Ours, too, live underground. They have queens. Some even engage in a form of agriculture, storing leaves on which they grow a sort of fungus. They have cows, which they milk.'

'Cows!'

'Well, they carry out raids on other insects, taking some home as prisoners. From them they extract a sweet substance. They fight with the greatest ferocity, and will defend their home to the death if it is attacked. And, of course, many are able to fly. So I repeat, these were perfectly ordinary ants, merely being larger than those to which we are accustomed, and having a corresponding degree of intelligence.'

'What about the formic acid?' asked Rex.

'It is a potent poison, which can be injected into their

enemies by their stings. You can try a little experiment when you get home. The next time you find an ants' nest, cut a stick and push it into the nest. Hold it there a minute; then pull it out and smell it. But be careful, because if the nest happens to be a strong one the result may surprise you.'

Gator broke into the conversation. 'Have you seen enough?'

'Yes, thank you.'

'Shall we depart?'

'By all means. This is one world I have no desire to revisit.'

'Then we will be on our way,' said Vargo, soberly. 'I hope, Professor, that this experience will encourage you to put a curb on your curiosity.'

'I doubt it,' murmured Tiger.

11 The ray

More food for thought was provided by a strange little world which, since it had no name, the Professor dubbed Aquania. Vargo, still intent on the main purpose of the voyage, which was to find Rolto, or from some other source gather news of the activities of Ardilla, would have passed without calling, but Borron made the mistake of mentioning some of the planet's peculiarities. When the Professor said: 'Aren't you going to call here?' and received a negative reply, he, of course, wanted to know why.

'We shan't find Rolto there,' said Vargo.

'How can you be sure of that?'

'Because I doubt if he could find a place to get down.'

'Why not?'

'For one very good reason.'

'Have you been there?'

'No, but I know the place by repute.'

The Professor turned to Borron. Indicating the planet which they were now passing he inquired, 'Have you been there?'

'No, but I once talked to a man of our fleet who did make a landing there. It was not from choice. He was having trouble with his ship, and some repair was needed that couldn't be carried out in flight.'

'Then it must be possible to land!'

'So it seems. He took a risk.' Borron glanced apologetically at Vargo.

'Come on, now. Why make a mystery of it?' pleaded the Professor. 'What's the trouble? Out with it.'

'The planet is practically all water.'

'Practically! Then there is *some* dry land.'

'The place is no more than a vast archipelago.'

'Do people live on the islands?'

'Men of a sort.'

'What do you mean by that?'

Borron made a gesture of resignation. 'The inhabitants are a human species but their habits are more like those of fish than men.'

'One would expect that if they live on a world that is mostly water,' asserted the Professor. 'I suppose, like other fish, they live on fish?'

'There isn't much else to eat.'

Toby shook his head. 'Is there *no* limit to the types that occupy the Universe?'

'Apparently not,' answered Vargo. 'Why should there be? Space is limitless and, as I have told you often enough, no two worlds are identical. The people, or other creatures, are what their world has made them. It could not be otherwise.'

The Professor agreed. 'Now we have got so far you might as well tell me all you know about this watery world.'

Vargo looked at Borron. 'You'd better tell him or we shall have no peace.'

'While we are talking you might take us closer Gator, even if we do not land,' requested the Professor. 'Proceed, please, with your story, Borron.'

'There is not much to tell,' began the old navigator. 'The people are small and brown. They have large hands and feet, with skin between their fingers and toes. I think I have heard you call this arrangement, in connection with certain birds that live on water, webbed feet.'

'That is correct. You don't mean fins – like fish?'

'No. But they may become fins in course of time if the present conditions persist long enough.'

'What are these conditions?'

'Rain. Always it rains. It is very hot so evaporation is excessive. The water falls back as rain. More water must come from somewhere else, too, because the level of the water is always rising. That has been going on for nobody knows how long. Gradually the land has become submerged, so now there is very little left, always in the form of islands, some large, some small.'

'Could this be due to the planet itself shrinking?'

'That is a possibility I had not considered. But certainly it rains for long periods at a time, without stopping. As the water rose, covering the land, the people built boats. More and more boats. But still there were not enough, and for short journeys the people took to swimming. Now, in the water, they can swim fast for great distances. Also they can swim far under water, without air. Their lungs have become large enough to hold the air, and their chests large to hold the lungs.'

'Wonderful!' cried the Professor. 'This seems to be a case of evolution, of adaptability, at its best.'

'They had to take more and more to swimming when the supply of wood for boats began to run out. With less land there was less wood. Now all wood is carefully preserved. Chiefly it is used to build houses, and large rafts on which to build more houses as the population increases. Some of the islands are not land at all, but enormous rafts on which houses have been built. They built houses on houses, one above the other. They do not really need boats now, because by swimming from island to island it is possible for a man to swim round the world. That, I was told, is often done, mostly for sport. They hold round-the-world races. As the air and water are always warm they do not need much in the way of clothes.'

'What do these people eat?' asked Rex.

'Fish is their chief diet. The water is full of fish.'

'Are they happy?'

'Quite happy. They have only one problem and that is always with them - the rising water.'

'So they are not hostile?'

'No, they are friendly.'

'I take it they have no spaceships?' queried the Professor.

Vargo answered the question. 'You will only find people scientifically advanced on the larger, older planets. On small planets where life exists the people are too taken up with problems of sheer survival to experiment with mechanical devices. I imagine you find that on certain areas of Earth.'

'Quite so,' returned the Professor. As long as the people can manage to live they seem content. They reach a point of physical development and there they stop. Their mentality does not rise above their physical requirements. Still, if they are satisfied with their lot what does it matter? Scientific advancement is not necessarily the road to that tranquillity of mind which we call happiness. Far from it, in fact. But pray continue, Borron.'

'There is really nothing more to say.'

'Is all this water fresh or salt?'

'Slightly salt. The old people say it is less salt than it used to be.'

'They are lucky there, anyway,' asserted Tiger. 'If ever the water becomes less, should evaporation ever exceed precipitation, the water, containing the same amount of salt, might become undrinkable. It might become so salt that swimming in it would become impossible. We have such a place, a large lake, on Earth, called the Dead Sea. It is too salty even for fish to live in it.'

'Should that happen on the place we've been talking about the people would be faced with starvation. They may not be aware of it.'

'Should all the fish die the smell would about finish the place,' put in Toby.

'A most unpleasant thought,' said the Professor, reprovingly.

Vargo continued. 'Well, now you know all about it I suppose you would like to go there.'

'I would, very much.' The Professor smiled. 'One day, when I write a book on my travels, it will shake the people of Earth to know what can happen to them. It should also make them well-satisfied with what they have, and perhaps restrain them from killing each other in wars.'

Vargo made a sign to Gator. 'Shall we have a look to see how these watermen are getting on?'

'Not now,' answered Gator. 'That could be left for another occasion. I would rather proceed with what we set out to do. If we are going to make diversions to call at every little planet that has unique features we shall never get to Terromagna, where Multavo will be expecting us. If we fail to arrive it is more than probable that he will start a search for us, and perhaps lose his ship, if not his life, in the process.'

'We were hoping to find Rolto,' reminded Rex.

'I cannot imagine him in any circumstances being on Aquania, as you call this wet little planet. It is much too far off the course he would take to reach the Terromagna constellation, which was his final objective, as it is ours.

'He would have heard of Aquania?'

'I imagine so, in which case he would know about the difficulty of finding a landing place there. We have wasted much time already, and our air supply is not unlimited.'

'I think you are right, Gator,' said the Professor. 'Our first duty is to investigate the menace of Ardilla, without indulging our curiosity in mere whims. Carry on for Terromagna.'

Nothing more was said for a little while as the *Tavona* cruised on, Gator and Borron keeping close watch on the glare of white light that marked the position of one of the great suns of the region. Already its heat could be felt in the ship.

Then Rex said: 'How far are we now from Ardilla?'

'Still a long way,' Borron told him. He pointed to a star of the first magnitude. 'There it is. Why do you ask?'

'I was wondering if they had already spotted us. I mean, if they had a sort of radar device like the interstellar television of Terromagna.'

'If we knew that, one of our questions would be answered,' said Vargo.

'Which one?'

'The effective range of their ray-projecting equipment. Were they able to see us, if we are within range we should have known about it by now.'

The Professor spoke. 'To me the vital question is whether Ardilla puts out a single ray, aiming it at any ship that approaches, or if it broadcasts its evil influence thus filling the entire region. I was thinking that if it puts out a single ray it might be possible to swerve out of it.'

'If it is able to keep the target in view it could follow it whichever way it turned.'

'In that case there could be no escape.'

'That could depend on how far we or the ship were incapacitated before we realized we were being attacked. It is my belief that Ardilla is able to project more than one sort of ray. We know of one sort that affects the brain for we have had experience of it.'

'Since they know we are not entirely defenceless they may not try that one again,' said Tiger, grimly.

'The scientists on Terromagna – I remember Multavo telling me – believe that Ardilla has concentrated on ray development and that they have several types at their disposal,' said Vargo. 'What they have actually done, of course, is gain control of some of the rays that are forever present in the Universe. On Earth you know of the existence of many, but as yet we know very little about them.'

Another silence fell. The ship cruised on.

After a time Gator said they were as near the sun as they dare go, which automatically meant that they were as far as they could get from Ardilla. Their air supply was not sufficient to take them round the far side of the sun, which would have meant a tremendous journey through unknown regions, to say nothing of occupying more time than was reasonable.

It was when Rex moved to wind up his watch that he discovered something was wrong, although he was not immediately aware of its significance. His head seemed perfectly clear, but his hand moved so slowly that he stared at it in surprise. In fact, he had some difficulty in moving it at all. He glanced at the others. They were sitting still, apparently normal, although, he realized, they may have had no occasion to move. He himself had felt quite comfortable until he had decided to wind his watch.

Unwilling to raise an alarm that might prove to be false he tried lifting his arm. It came up, slowly, but the movement required a definite effort. His fingers, he noticed, were trembling, although at this stage that was certainly not from fear. His legs had pins-and-needles. He tried to get up, but his body seemed to weigh a ton. What was the matter with him, he wondered desperately. Was he ill? Had he been stricken with paralysis? Was the pressure in the ship failing? Had Gator suddenly decided to accelerate? He opened his mouth to ask him: or, it would be more correct to say, he tried to. But his jaws were clamped tight. He forced them apart, only to discover that his tongue was frozen, so that the only sound he could make was a choking, strangled cry.

He saw the others begin to turn to look at him, and saw from the expressions on their faces they had discovered they were suffering in the same way. They were still able to move, but so slowly that it was like looking at a picture in slow-motion.

He watched with an awful fascination as Gator's hand crept at a snail's pace to the controls: saw the muscles of his face become taut with the effort required. What he was trying to do he did not know. All he knew, or by this time suspected, was that one of the dreaded rays had got them in its grip. After that he was not entirely clear about what was happening, for his ears were ringing and his sight was failing. The picture was now out of focus, and fading.

After what seemed to be a long time, during which he could only sit as if frozen to his seat, he saw the scene begin to clear; saw the others making slow movements as if to test their limbs; saw a slow smile twist Gator's face, usually set in a taciturn expression. He had an extraordinary sensation of life beginning to flow into his veins, and presently gulped with relief when he found he was almost back to normal.

As the unseen power continued to diminish he said: 'Did you—feel it?'

The others assured him that they had.

'It was the ray.'

'I don't know what else it could have been,' answered the Professor.

'We've escaped.'

'So it seems.'

'But how did we do it?'

'I have an idea Gator could answer that,' said Tiger. 'The last thing I saw he was doing something to the controls.'

The Professor looked at Gator. 'What did you do?'

'I raced the ray.'

'You *what*?'

'I out-distanced the ray.'

'You mean, you dodged out of it?'

'I tried to, but failed.'

'Then what *did* you do?'

'As I have said, I raced the ray. It is true I turned back over our course, a wide turn that took us dangerously near the sun. You may have felt the heat. Then I went away from Ardilla at maximum velocity.'

'But I still don't see what good that would do. You would still be in the path of the ray.'

'I am not a ray expert, but since we started on this trip I have thought a lot about them,' said Gator. 'At least, I thought about those of which we have knowledge. I remembered that all rays, like an electric current – which after all is only a ray even if it is carried on a wire – have a definite velocity. Some travel fast, others comparatively slowly. I imagine it depends on the wave-length. The question that sprang to my mind, when I realized we were in the grip of a ray, was, what was its velocity? If it travelled faster than the *Tavona* we were lost. But if we could travel faster than the ray there was a chance of escape. We were only cruising, you remember, when the ray caught us. Having turned I put the ship into its maximum velocity, as quickly as I dared and the experiment succeeded. As we approached the velocity of the ray its power began to diminish. By the time I was in absolute maximum the ray had lost its force. In other words, we had out-run it.'

'Are we still in it?'

'We may be. Or it may be following us. Either way, as long as we are travelling the faster it can't hurt us.'

'By the same argument, should we turn and fly into it, we would again feel the effect.'

'The effect, I think would be worse, because we should receive the full force of it. The faster we went the more devastating would be the result. I imagine we would be unable to move a muscle, in which case we should hurtle straight down the ray into Ardilla; or, assuming the ray is under control, in any direction the operators should care to send us.'

'That is a wonderful piece of information,' declared the Professor. 'The first piece of authentic news we have had of the limitations of the rays. It seems that as a weapon they are not invincible after all. Allow me to congratulate you, my dear Gator, on a brilliant piece of deduction. It occurs to me that we should carry it a little farther, while we have the opportunity'

Everyone looked startled.

'We've escaped! Isn't that enough?' cried Tiger.

'The more we can learn about this murderous device the better for everyone. Other lives, as well as our own, may depend upon it.'

'What do you want me to do?' asked Gator.

'Test your theory in practice. Reduce our velocity—'

'*What*?' almost shouted Tiger and Rex together.

Only until the first effect of the ray is felt,' explained the Professor quickly. 'As soon as we are aware of the first symptoms of paralysis all we have to do is return to maximum velocity. In that way, judging from the moment all such symptoms disappear, we could determine the velocity of the ray. That information passed on to other ships would enable them to know at what velocity they would be safe. Any ship not having the necessary velocity would be asking for trouble to venture into the region of Ardilla.'

'That would apply only to this particular ray,' Gator pointed out. 'There is reason to believe Ardilla has several.'

'Still, it would be something gained,' persisted the Professor. 'In my opinion, for what it is worth, all these rays may be operated by the same power unit, in which case what could apply to one could apply to all.'

'I understand what you mean,' said Gator. 'I will make the test. Sit still, everyone. We may not all have exactly the same reactions, so the first person to feel anything please cry out.'

'You can bet I will,' stated Tiger, warmly.

Actually, Toby was the first to feel the effect of the ray. Rex had not been conscious of any change in the ship's velocity, but it must have dropped, for at the precise moment that Toby made his cry he felt the first warning tightening of his muscles. The feeling passed as Gator resumed maximum speed.

'Capital!' exclaimed the Professor. 'So now we know. That little experiment may be the means of saving millions of lives, perhaps whole worlds of people.'

'A thought has just struck me,' said Rex.

'What is it? No more experiments, I hope,' said Tiger.

'No. But if Rolto came this way, and this is the direction he said he intended to take, he would feel the effect of the ray exactly as we did.'

'Well?'

'If that was so one of two things must have happened. If he could think of no way to escape he must by now be a dead man But if the same thought struck him as struck Gator he would have acted in the same way, in which case he must be somewhere directly in front of us.'

'That was very well worked out, my boy,' said the Professor.

'It could be,' agreed Vargo. 'As a captain of his flight Rolto was a man of great knowledge and experience.'

'He may have gone down on the planet I see looming up in front of us,' returned the Professor, thoughtfully.

'It is possible,' agreed Vargo.

'Then let us go and have a look at it. If I am any judge of distance it will not take us far out of our way.'

'I could do with a breath of fresh air, anyhow,' declared Tiger.

'Very well,' said Vargo. 'We will see if Rolto is there.'

'I shall be surprised if he is,' remarked Borron.

The Professor's eyebrows went up. 'Why? Do you know this planet?'

Borron looked slightly amused. 'Yes, I know it. We are going back over our course. What you see is the watery world we decided to miss – the one you called Aquania.'

'Ah! You think there would be difficulty in finding a place to land?'

'That will be the trouble,' confirmed Borron.

12 Mostly water

It may well be said at once that they did not find Rolto on Aquania. But they learned from the webfooted inhabitants that a ship painted with blue stars had been there for a short time. As this described Rolto's spacecraft it was safe to conclude that he had been there, having presumably retired there for the same reason as themselves. To escape the Ardilla ray. The people of Aquania knew nothing about this.

It seemed that Rolto and his crew had been more seriously affected than they had, for according to the natives some of them were ill on arrival, having partly lost the use of their limbs. As Toby remarked, they had either received a much stronger dose of the ray or had been subject to it for a longer period, with the result that the effects had taken longer to wear off. Those in the *Tavona* had been conscious of a slight stiffness for an hour or two, but then it had worn off, and by the time they were nearing their new objective they were back to normal.

As Gator took the ship down with even more than customary care, Borron, who was watching the surface of the planet, observed that there did not seem to be as much water as he had been led to expect – at all events, on the side they were approaching. There was, as everyone could see, plenty of water there, and a great many small islands that were obviously occupied. But there were also a large number of low, flat islands, some of fair size, which, from their colour and the fact that they supported no vegetation of any sort, looked as if they might be sand-banks.

It turned out that this was what they were. There was not a soul on any of them, which struck Rex as odd, because he could see people swarming on the beaches of the islands on which their fantastic piles of wooden houses had been built.

'Something must have happened here,' said Borron, as the ship hovered preparatory to landing.

'Surely only one thing could have happened,' said Toby. 'There is less water than formerly, with the result that the shallows are now dry land.'

'Where could the water have gone? Tell me that,' invited the Professor. 'It must still be somewhere on the planet. A world can't get rid of its water.'

'You said it would become brine if—'

'Only by excessive evaporation,' broke in the Professor.

'In which case the fish, the staple food here, would die.'

'That does not appear to have happened,' observed Vargo.

'Very strange,' murmured the Professor. 'It seems that we have yet another problem to solve.'

'I know one thing,' put in Tiger. 'It must be pretty warm here. I can feel the ship warming up. The water must be tepid.'

Had Gator circumnavigated the globe the problem might have been solved forthwith; but having no reason to do so he went straight on down and made his landing on a long broad sand-bank close to one of the larger inhabited islands.

'One would have thought,' remarked the Professor, as the usual atmospheric tests were being made, 'that the people here would have relieved their congested areas by occupying some of these new islands. At least, I assume they are new. Of course, there must be a reason for that. Presently we may find out what it is.'

'What is even more strange, they do not appear even to visit them,' put in Vargo. 'Be careful, Gator. I have a feeling that things here are not quite what they appear to be.'

'Here comes the natives now, anyway,' said Tiger, as scores of people plunged into the intervening lagoon and raced across the placid water at a speed that was wonderful to behold. They might have been a fleet of torpedoes.

They reached the ship just as those in it stepped out into a heat that was breath-taking. Rex, having been told what to expect, looked at the little brown men more with amusement then surprise. With their abnormal chests, and webbed extremities, they reminded him of frogs. They were obviously more at home in the water than on land, where they moved clumsily, their broad feet often getting in the way. However, they seemed friendly enough, and did not appear to be in the least surprised by the arrival of a spaceship. Indeed, they hardly looked at it. And far from falling silent with amazement they set up a terrific chattering, all talking at once, pointing and waving, not at the ship, as might have been expected, but at the horizon. That they were in a state of high excitement was plain, although for what reason was not evident.

'What's all the fuss about?' said the Professor. 'Clearly, we are not the first visitors here from space. They've seen ships like this before. They're trying to tell us something. Vargo, can you find what it is?'

Vargo made a gesture of helplessness. 'They can't speak our language and we don't know theirs, so we are up against the usual difficulty. But I have a feeling that they are trying to warn us of some danger.'

'It seems pretty urgent, too,' put in Tiger.

The Professor looked around, 'It's hard to see what danger there could be here, unless there is some sort of beast in the water.'

'The ground seems firm, so we are not on a quicksand, or anything like that,' contributed Toby.

'I wonder could it be anything to do with that?' surmised Rex, indicating a large moon, the rim of which had crept up over the horizon. 'It seems to be the chief object of interest,' he added. 'They keep pointing at it.'

Borron answered. 'The man who described the place to me

said nothing about a moon. But satellites are so common everywhere in the region of planets that one would hardly be worth remarking. Of course, the one we see may be a new arrival. Or it might not have been so close when my friend was here. If it is new, that could account for the excitement.'

'The arrival of another moon would cause some excitement on Earth,' said Rex, smiling at such a whimsical notion.

'Please be silent while I try to put some questions,' requested Vargo. Going up to one of the most intelligent-looking natives he resorted to sign language. The man got the idea at once. His companions, which included some small boys who looked hardly old enough to walk, never mind swim, gathered round to watch the performance.

The awkward method of conversation went on for some time, during which, Rex noticed, the natives threw frequent glances at the moon which, although it was broad daylight, could be seen – still rising; which gave some indication of its size, and the power of the sun, the light of which it was reflecting. Not that he needed to be told about the sun. The heat it was hurling down was little short of blistering, and he had to keep his handkerchief in use to mop the perspiration that trickled down his face.

'Well, what do you make of it?' the Professor asked Vargo, after a time.

Vargo revealed as much as he had been able to gather. It was not much. Another ship, like their own, had been there recently. It had blue stars on its side so it could only have been Rolto. Some of the men had been sick. They moved slowly and with difficulty. The ship left in a great hurry.

'What I can't understand is why the ship left in such a hurry,' admitted Vargo. 'At first the crew behaved as if they were going to stay until they were fully recovered. The people here gave them food. Then, for some reason, they went off and did not return. That's as much as I can make of it.'

'I thought that man seemed to be inviting us to go to his village,' said the Professor.

'Oh, yes. They are amiable enough.'

Gator stepped in. 'Since Rolto would not rush away without good reason we had better be prepared to do the same thing,' he cautioned.

'I think I know what caused his sudden departure!' exclaimed Rex, in a flash of inspiration. 'Look!' He pointed. 'Is that the tide coming in?'

He had for some minutes been watching a long white line form right along the horizon, his attention having been drawn to it by the behaviour of some of the natives, who were looking at it, not exactly with fear but certainly with anxiety and mounting apprehension. The line was rapidly getting brighter, more distinct.

They all gazed at it, natives and visitors alike.

'That's water,' decided Tiger. 'Never mind the tide coming in, from the speed it's travelling it looks to me more like a tidal wave.'

'That would explain everything, the behaviour of the natives and why Rolto left in haste,' said Vargo. 'The wave is coming this way.'

'We had better get aboard,' advised Borron.

Even now none of them realized the necessity for urgency, for the wave was still many miles away; as it was agreed afterwards, they should have done, for more and more natives were taking to the water and streaking to their village.

'Yes, I think we'd better be ready to move,' said the Professor. 'What a nuisance. I would have liked to see more of these fishy people.'

Those of the *Tavona's* crew who had stepped out began to file back in. They started in a leisurely way, but finished with a rush as the truth became all too clear.

A high wall of green water with a white curling crest, stretching the full width of the horizon, was bearing down on them at the speed of an express train. And suddenly it was making nearly as much noise as one. From being distant it was now too close to be believed. There was not even time to close the *Tavona's* doors.

As the Professor, who as usual was last, having turned for a final look at the phenomenon, tumbled inside, Gator took off. For a dreadful moment Rex thought it was all over with them, for one of the ship's legs stuck in the soft sand into which it had sunk a little way. It came clear just in time, and the ship rose at an angle that sent everyone in it rolling across the floor. The Professor nearly fell out, and would have done had not Tiger grabbed him by the leg.

The top of the wave must have missed the ship by a matter of inches, for by the time Rex was on his feet, and had scrambled to a window, the sand-bank was no longer there. What had been dry sand was now a tossing, turbulent flood.

'No wonder Rolto left in a hurry,' muttered Tiger, when they had recovered from the shock. 'He must nearly have been caught the same way. Another few seconds and we would have been like King John in the Wash – up the creek without a paddle.'

'And there is the villain who was responsible,' cried the Professor, pointing to the moon, now a gigantic orb clear of the horizon. 'Why did nobody realize that a body that size was bound to drag the water with it, producing a colossal tide which, over a flat surface, would travel at frightful speed? Dear, dear. I must be getting half-witted in my old age.'

'The inhabited islands seem to have escaped,' observed Toby, as they looked down from a safe altitude.

'No doubt they were chosen for that reason, and the houses constructed to withstand the assault should the water reach them,' answered the Professor. 'It is no matter for wonder, either, that the inhabitants of this unlucky little world have developed semiaquatic bodies and limbs. They must spend half their lives in the water, or dodging it.'

'What a place to live, with that sort of thing going on,' said Rex. 'Have you noticed that wherever we go something unpleasant seems to happen to make life difficult?'

'It seems to me that there are few places where life is as easy as it is on Earth,' opined Toby.

'As far as Aquania is concerned it is unlikely that the people worry much about the tides,' replied the Professor. 'This is their way of life, and they probably imagine that every other world has the same problem to face. It may not be as bad as it seems to us. What we have just seen must be a regular occurrence, and the people had adapted themselves to it. They knew what was going to happen, and it is clear now that they did their best to warn us. How often the flood tide occurs must depend, of course, on the course taken by the moon, which from its size is able to drag the water behind it from one side of the planet to the other. After all, the same thing happens on Earth, although fortunately for us to a lesser extent. We have made provision to deal with high and low tides. Had they been worse than they are, no doubt we should still have been able to make allowances for them. Once the people knew what to expect, and when, there was no longer any danger. Now the tides are tabulated, although it is not unknown for careless people to be caught by them. For that there is no longer any excuse, although long ago, in the days of ignorance, there may have been.

'History records many such accidents,' the Professor went on. 'Exceptional tides and tidal waves can still cause mischief, but Earth can consider itself fortunate that it doesn't have the sort of tides the people below have to face. I don't think we need go back.' The Professor turned to Gator. 'Where would be the most likely place for Rolto to make for when he left here?'

'It's hard to say He would probably carry on towards

Terromagna; but he wouldn't feel like taking another chance with the ray that drove him off his course.'

'Neither do we,' put in Tiger, grimly.

'What would he do to avoid the ray?' asked the Professor.

Borron consulted his chart. 'He might make a dash for Dacoona. That would take him out of the way, but he would avoid the danger area.'

'Dacoona! Isn't that the place where the people sleep long and live longer?'

'Yes. If, as we suppose, Rolto discovered that he could out-distance the ray, he would be reasonably safe in making for that planet. On feeling the first symptoms he would only have to travel at maximum velocity.'

The Professor looked pensive, and perhaps a little dubious. 'That the paralysis ray can be raced is a major discovery, but it doesn't really solve the Ardilla problem, you know. The danger remains. Ardilla still rules the region. Ships can only survive by running away from it.'

'Which goes against the grain,' growled Tiger.

'We will hear what Terromagna has to say about it,' concluded Vargo.

The *Tavona* sped on through space, with the tide-menaced little world of Aquania resuming its customary appearance in the distant sky.

'I see something ahead of us,' said the Professor, after some time had passed in silence. 'What is the next planet on our line of flight, Borron?'

The navigator referred to his chart. 'There is a planet. A small one. It is unknown to me. It has not been given a name so I imagine none of our people has been there.'

'Another unknown planet, eh?'

'There are millions of planets still unknown. It would not be possible to find names for all of them. It was not easy to find names for all the constellations. The planet we see in front of us is a lonely one. There is nothing else near it.'

'Rolto might be here,' said the Professor, reflectively.

Rex winked at his father, well aware that to the Professor the word unknown was like gold to a prospector.

'Rolto might be anywhere,' said Vargo.

'In which case he might be on the little world in front of us.'

'It is possible.'

'Then I suggest we have a look at it – just a glance, as it were, in passing.'

'We will, as you say, have a glance,' agreed Vargo. 'But it will be no more than a glance. We have wasted much time already.'

'Exploration is never a waste of time,' contended the Professor.

Vargo said no more.

13 Rulers in feathers

'What's on your mind?' Tiger put the question to Rex who for some time had sat gazing out of the window, at nothing in particular, lost in thought.

'There seems to be plenty to think about,' answered Rex, wrinkling his forehead. 'I can't help wondering why Ardilla should go out of its way, without any provocation, to hurt innocent travellers. On most of the planets we've visited, where there was a population that had reached the Scientific Age, we have found the people friendly and glad to see us. Why should Ardilla be different?'

'That is a question impossible to answer without making contact with them, and that, for obvious reasons, no one is in a hurry to attempt,' replied Vargo. 'It may be that it is not as civilized as indications suggest. Again, it could be that, like children with a new toy, it amuses them to try it out on someone. On the other hand, the Ardillans may be a super-race with Universal conquest in view.'

'One would think one world would be enough.'

'Not for some people,' interposed Tiger. 'It is said that Alexander, the Macedonian king, having conquered most of the land known on Earth, sat down and wept because he had no more worlds to conquer.'

'A good thing he didn't have a spaceship,' murmured Vargo.

'It may be there is a tyrant on Ardilla who suffers from the same complaint – vanity and ambition. Lust for power. Such men are a menace wherever they may be,' declared the Professor.

'Ardilla hasn't tried invading anyone yet,' put in Rex.

'Not as far as we know,' said Vargo 'Perhaps that will

come later, when they have perfected their weapons. They may be only in the experimental stage. If so, no doubt they will improve them, because that happens with all inventions and devices.'

'I don't know about that,' said Rex dubiously. 'We do know from our own experience that they have more than one ray. We also know they can be mobile, mounted in spaceships. The last time we ran into trouble they used a ray that had the power of causing one mind to link up with another, to the confusion of everyone under its influence. That ray attacked the brain. This time they used one that had the effect of paralysing the muscles. How do they do it?'

'I've been thinking about that,' resumed the Professor. 'I feel sure that all these rays have an electronic base. On Earth, you know, scientists are exploring the enormous potentialities of electronics. These confounded rays may derive from induction, or some form of it.'

'In what way?' asked Tiger.

'You, as an engineer, must know that if an alternating electric current is passed through a coil of wire, called the primary, and another coil, called the secondary, is wound round it, the secondary will be influenced without any metallic connection. This is called induction, as opposed to conduction.'

'Like the thing we used to amuse ourselves with called a "shocking" coil,' suggested Rex.

'Exactly. The greater the number of winds on the secondary, the higher the voltage; but since you don't get something for nothing, the lower becomes the amperage. The principle can be employed in the ignition system of internal combustion engines.'

'Coming back to these rays,' rejoined Vargo. 'According to Multavo, the belief of the leading scientists on Terromagna is that they exist externally everywhere; but they are soon dissipated, and therefore become too weak to have any marked effect. It is only when concentrated that they are noticeable. As we saw demonstrated when we were at Terromagna, the experts there have succeeded in tapping and selecting them, so that they can be used as a good or evil influence.'

'You think the Ardillans can do this, and have in fact developed the process?' asked the Professor.

'That is what the electronics specialist on Terromagna believe. But how they are able to send them out on a beam of such concentration, over such a great distance, remains to be discovered.'

'From what I know about electricity, if this theory is correct it should not be a very difficult matter to suppress them,' said Tiger thoughtfully.

'You are thinking of a condenser?' queried the Professor.

'Yes. One that can be attached to a ship. In such a device the rays should discharge themselves, in the same way that a suppressor will prevent interference in television.'

'Wouldn't the ray have to be suppressed at source?' asked Rex.

'Not necessarily. Anyway, the only protection I can envisage must be something of that sort.'

'The scientist of Terromagna, who are working on the problem, may produce such a device,' asserted Vargo. 'They are also considering a scheme for soaking Ardilla with its own rays. It is to be hoped they succeed, or space travel in the Third Region will come to a standstill.'

The *Tavona* flashed on, with Rex pondering on the conversation he had just heard, ideas which not so long ago would have sounded like pure fantasy. But not now. He was beginning to accept, without turning a hair, what once would have seemed to border on the miraculous. Again it struck him that the latent forces within the Universe were terrifying in their awful immensity.

They were now in free fall towards the unknown, unnamed planet. As they gazed down on it the Professor remarked: 'That looks quite a nice place. Not unlike a smaller edition of Mars.'

'There is no human form of life there,' observed Vargo. 'We should by now be seeing the unmistakable signs of occupation, the usual dwellings and roads between them.'

'It looks somewhat dry. I can see a lot of desert terrain,' said Tiger.

'It will be interesting to see what the atmosphere is like,' returned Vargo. 'We'll do that first, because should there be no air it would be a waste of time to look for Rolto there.'

The *Tavona* continued on down, and from a low altitude, with Borron making the atmospheric tests, made several trips round the unknown world. He reported that the air was dense, and carried a rather high content of carbon dioxide. It was breathable in small quantities, but he advised spacesuits should a landing be made.

'There is no point in landing,' said Vargo. 'Rolto is not here. There is no animal life, either.'

'I'm sorry, Vargo, but I'm afraid you're wrong for once,' asserted Rex. 'Those white things over the open ground below us can only be birds. Anyway, whatever they are they're in the air. I can see their shadows moving on that area of sandy stuff.'

'I think we might land, if only for a few minutes,' suggested the Professor. 'It is always pleasant to be able to take a little exercise, after being cooped up in the ship. Besides, I feel sure that if a specialized creature like a bird has developed here there must be other forms of life.'

'As you wish,' agreed Vargo. 'We can take the opportunity to clean up the ship.'

As the *Tavona* touched down several white birds that had been standing about took off and flapped heavily away. They were not very big, perhaps a little larger than herring gulls. Nobody took much notice of them, although the Professor remarked that it was surprising to find birds there. In their travels, the least common form of life had been feathered creatures. Nowhere had they seen such a variety of bird life as occurred on Earth, although why this should be had often been a subject for debate.

Rex was more interested in a number of holes, fairly large holes, each with a mound of soil outside it in the manner of a rabbit burrow. Indeed, a piece of rising ground had the appearance of a rabbit warren, although the size of the holes suggested an animal a good deal larger than a rabbit.

'There's something else here besides birds,' he remarked, as he put on his spacesuit. 'At least, I can't imagine birds digging those holes.'

'There are a few birds that live in holes in the ground,' reminded Tiger.

'Why should the birds here live in holes?' questioned the Professor. 'As far as I can see they've nothing to fear. What does strike me as odd is that the things that live in holes are all underground. One would have expected a few to show themselves. But of course, the answer may be that they are nocturnal in their habit.'

'I'm having nothing to do with holes,' declared Tiger. 'We've barged into one on this trip, and that was enough for me. I shan't forget those ants in a hurry.'

'Whatever lives in these must be too small to do us any harm,' rejoined the Professor, confidently.

'I've just seen something move at the mouth of one of those holes,' said Rex. 'It peeped out, then popped back inside.'

'What did it look like?'

'I didn't see much of it, but the head looked rather like that of a monkey. A chimpanzee.'

'Wait a minute before you open the doors, Vargo,'

requested the Professor. 'Perhaps one of them will show itself.'

They waited for about five minutes. Then Tiger said: 'Nothing doing. They're not coming out. They're scared of us.'

Rex glanced up at the birds that were wheeling about. 'So are the birds, apparently,' he observed.

'Strange,' murmured the Professor. 'Creatures unaccustomed to seeing human beings are rarely afraid of them. Fear comes later, when they learn that men are not to be trusted. Open the doors, Vargo, please, and we'll stretch our legs outside.'

The doors were opened, and heavy, sultry air poured into the ship. The Professor stepped out, followed by Tiger, Toby and Rex, to find the gravity rather unbalancing, as they knew from the size of the planet it would be. The birds were still gliding about, high overhead, on rigid pinions.

The Professor walked on a few paces and then stopped to look around, and, no doubt, to get used to the slight gravity. Rex, who hated the spacesuit that restricted movement, hoped he would not go far.

'Those birds are coming lower,' remarked Tiger, casually.

'To have a look at the strange mortals from Earth, no doubt,' replied the Professor, with a chuckle. 'Let us watch them for a minute. Their development, should there be any peculiarities, may give us an idea of conditions here.'

'I say! By Jove! Look at that!' exclaimed Rex, as one of the birds folded its wings and plummeted down like a stone.

'A pretty piece of dive bombing, although I can't see the target,' observed Tiger.

'It's coming close. We should get a good view of it when it flattens out,' stated the Professor, adjusting his spectacles.

That they themselves might be the target was a possibility that obviously did not occur to any of them, for they stood still, gazing up at what was without doubt a fine example of aerobatics. Only at the last moment, when it looked as if the bird might collide with one of them, did they jump aside, and even then Rex put the performance down to accident rather than design. But when the bird which, with curved beak and talons, suddenly looked more like an eagle, flashed past, and came round in a superbly executed turn before going into another dive, its purpose became plain.

'Look out!' shouted Rex. 'It's after us.'

Vargo also shouted from the door of the ship. Rex caught the words 'up above.' Looking up he saw a dozen or more birds coming down. Whistling wings made him turn, and as he ducked, the original bird missed him by inches. Instinctively he struck at it, and knocked a few feathers out of a wing tip.

By this time, realizing what was happening, everyone was in full retreat, blundering towards the ship. With the vibrating whirr of wings in their ears they managed to reach it without anyone actually being struck, although there were some near misses. They clambered in, and on this occasion not even the Professor lingered for a last look. The doors slammed. But even now the birds did not call off the attack. There was a crash as one hit the ship and plastered a window with a horrid welter of blood and feathers. Another and another dashed itself to pieces against the hard shell of the ship in the fury of its attack. More birds were coming from all directions.

'You'd better get off,' Tiger told Gator, as he removed his headpiece. 'Those infernal birds are doing the ship no good. By thunder! No wonder the monkeys live underground. Anything would have to, here, with these lunatics in feathers always on the prowl.'

'Yes, I would say they are the dominant species,' said the Professor. 'Of course, we have some fearless birds on Earth, notably the great white condor of the Andes. They have been known to attack men. Fortunately they are not common. The strength of this species lies in its numbers. With a gun one might be able to deal with one bird, or even two or three. But against such a flock as this, even you, my dear Group-Captain, would be helpless.'

'With a few good loaders round me I wouldn't mind having a go at 'em,' growled Tiger.

'I don't think we'll bother about it today,' decided Vargo. 'Let us be on our way. And I suggest we make no more of these casual calls until we have seen Multavo and asked him what is to be done about Ardilla.'

14 The project

On the long run to Terromagna Rex had plenty of time for reflection, since Vargo refused to be moved from his decision to make no more calls on the way. So the Professor could only gaze and speculate on the constellations through which they passed as they travelled on to the Outer Galaxy.

There were a few minutes of anxiety when, in spite of the tremendous detour they were making, they experienced the 'pins-and-needles' sensation of stiffening muscles which told them that even now they were not outside the range of Ardilla's ray weapons. However, Gator took evasive action by running away from the beam at maximum velocity, and, as before, this method of escape succeeded. There was no other incident. With the peril evaded the ship's company settled down again, and Rex resumed the reverie from which he had been aroused. He found that whatever he tried to do to pass the time he invariably lapsed into a state that was not quite sleep yet not full consciousness. It might be called being 'lost in thought,'

In deep meditation it seemed to him that the worlds they had visited fell into groups, subdivided into those where conditions appeared to be static, and those which were either making progress or deteriorating. Where there was life, that particular world was dominated, naturally, by the most influential form, whether it happened to be animal, insect, reptile, or even, in one or two rare cases, vegetable; but where the form was human, even though it might be primitive, it took command.

Where there was any kind of civilization it was always in process of change, either having passed its peak, or still making progress towards – what? A better life? A higher civilization?

Only on a few of the planets they had seen was there anything comparable with Earth. The great exception, although there might be others in the remote regions of the Universe, was Terromagna, for which they were now heading. They had been there before, to be amazed by its wonders, so they knew what to expect.

Another obviously scientifically advanced world was Ardilla, although as far as was known no one had been there. This planet had gone its own way, and was now regarded by space travellers as something of an outlaw. Earth, with its almost ideal conditions of atmosphere and temperature, was on its way to becoming another Terromagna. It might take a thousand years, or ten thousand, according to the behaviour of the inhabitants. By a misuse of its knowledge it could destroy itself. That was the danger.

As the Professor had more than once remarked, the people at home did not realize how lucky they were. They lived on a world that was constant, in a solar system where there was little if any change. It had one moon that was always with them. These things had enabled them to divide their time with absolute precision into years, months, weeks, days, hours and even seconds. Short of an astronomical disaster these conditions were likely to go on indefinitely.

Rex dismissed these ponderous thoughts and roused himself from his lethargy when his father told him they had arrived and were going down on Terromagna.

'We shall soon know if Multavo is there,' said Vargo. 'If he is he will be waiting for us. The watchers on duty in the observatory will have seen us coming.'

His prediction was soon confirmed. Even before the *Tavona* touched down on the busy central landing-ground Mutavo could be seen standing there beside his sleek, silent conveyance. Rex's eyes went over the several spaceships present, but they were all interconstellation regular service types. Rolto's blue-starred Minoan ship was not among them.

When they stepped out, to sway a trifle unsteadily after their long voyage, Vargo's first words to Multavo were: 'Is Rolto here?'

'No,' he was told.

'You've neither seen nor heard anything of him?'

'Not a sight or a sound. He hasn't been within sight of our observation stations.'

'We called at several places on our way here but failed to find him,' said Vargo.

'It looks bad.'

'I'm afraid he must have become another on Ardilla's list of victims. Rolto was brave, but inclined to be reckless and take chances.'

'You yourselves had trouble I believe,' said Multavo. 'We were watching you on the telescopic long-distance interstellar screen and saw you suddenly change direction.'

'Yes,' answered Vargo. 'We ran into a paralysis ray which nearly overcame us; but Gator used his head and managed to evade the beam by going into top velocity and racing it.'

'Very good. We tried to get a message to you, to warn you to keep away from Dacoona. We thought you might call there, but fortunately you did not.'

Vargo frowned. 'Has something happened there?'

'We're afraid so. We have tried repeatedly to contact them but they have gone silent. We think the ray may have reached them.'

'That is bad news. Haven't you been able to find the answer to the Ardilla menace?'

'Come to my house,' invited Mutavo quietly. 'Your rooms are ready. We will talk there.'

'You didn't answer Vargo's question,' said the Professor,

anxiously, as Multavo took them to his home in one of the official vehicles. 'Can you or can you not prevent Ardilla putting out these devastating rays? To us that is a vital question. One day we shall want to go home, and if nothing can be done about these rays, which may increase their range, the sooner we start the better chance we shall have of getting through.'

'The question is not so vital to you as it is to us,' asserted Multavo. 'We are closer to the danger area. Since you demand a direct answer, it must be no, we cannot prevent Ardilla from discharging these rays.'

The Professor's face fell. 'Oh dear! That is terrible news.'

'Not so bad as it may sound,' returned Multavo, vaguely, as he pulled up in the flower-filled garden of his house. 'Come in and have some refreshment. Afterwards I will tell you something.'

An hour later, after a simple but satisfying meal, the conversation was resumed in what Multavo called his rest room.

'Now,' he began, when he had seen that his guests were comfortable. 'I am reluctant to raise hopes that may not be fulfilled, but—'

'You said you couldn't prevent Ardilla shooting out its rays,' interposed Rex, looking slightly bewildered.

'That is true. Neither can we. But we may have found a way of confining them within certain limits. As you may have learned on Earth, every weapon has produced a counter-weapon. What we purpose doing is the result of a long series of experiments by our leading atomic and electronic experts.'

'Of which, I believe, you are one,' put in Vargo.

'I have helped,' agreed Multavo, modestly.

'I see,' said the Professor, thoughtfully. 'You can't stop the rays being put out, but you can make them ineffective. Is that it?'

'Not exactly. But we shall, it is hoped, prevent them from reaching far into space. If they could be confined to the proximity of Ardilla itself, neither we, nor you, nor anyone else, would have anything to fear from them.'

'Quite so.'

'We might even do more than that,' went on Multavo. 'Let me try to give you a broad idea of what we intend to do. I cannot avoid certain technicalities, but we will keep The Project, as the experiment is officially called, in terms as simple as possible. If I do not make myself clear on any point do not hesitate to stop me. Smoke that poisonous weed you carry, Group-Captain, if you wish.'

'Thanks,' acknowledged Tiger, taking pipe and pouch from his pocket. 'It may be imagination but I fancy tobacco helps me to think.'

'If you cannot exercise your mind without what is evidently a narcotic it is a weakness to be deplored,' asserted Multavo.

'Yet you confess to a liking of our other narcotic – tea.'

'I would hardly call that a narcotic although I must admit it has habit-forming properties,' replied Multavo. 'But let us not argue about that now. Narcotics will not answer our present problem. This is The Project. But first, a question. I assume you all have some knowledge of how and why your internal radio communication system works on Earth?'

The listeners assured him that they had.

'Very well. Then you will know that radio communication is made possible by means of layers of ionized gas which form in the upper atmosphere. These reflect downwards the radio waves which have travelled upwards. Some travel horizontally across the surface of the planet, but these become too attenuated by metallic and other structures to serve any useful purpose.'

'We call one of these layers the Heaviside Layer, after the man who discovered it, Professor Heaviside,' informed Tiger.

'So,' continued Multavo. 'Now, these rays which Ardilla is putting out are in the form of electromagnetic waves; or at least they have a similar characteristic in the matter of reflection. There is without doubt what you would call a Heaviside Layer in the upper atmosphere of Ardilla, because such layers are common to all planets that have an atmosphere. You may wonder, therefore, why the Ardilla rays are not reflected back upon the surface of that planet, in the same way that ordinary radio waves bounce back.'

'That thought did occur to me,' said the Professor.

'The answer,' informed Multavo, 'is this. Wavelengths of less than ten metres are able to penetrate the Layer. They go right through it. Which means that as far as very short waves are concerned the Layer might as well not be there.'

'And Ardilla is using such short waves?'

'Yes. We were soon able to confirm that. Hence their range. They go straight into Outer Space. Could *anything* stop them? This was the root of the problem with which we were faced. What was needed was a medium that *would* deflect these short waves. In other words, arrest them and hurl them back at the transmitters. If that could be done the rays would never reach Outer Space. Do I make myself clear?'

'Perfectly clear,' replied the Professor. 'Have you found such a medium?'

'We think so.'

'Have you tried it yet?'

'No. Where could such a test be made? On ourselves? On our friends, and perhaps do irreparable damage?'

The Professor adjusted his spectacles and pushed back his lank front hair. 'As I understand it, what you hope to do is surround Ardilla with an artificial Layer which the rays would be unable to penetrate.'

'Exactly.'

'Forgive me if I say that seems an impossible undertaking. The volume of the medium required would be too enormous. And, besides, what is going to happen to the people detailed to lay this fantastic barrage? How could they do it without falling victim to the rays?'

'That, of course, was the next problem. How to do it without human agency. We could hardly ask our operators to commit suicide by going within the known range of Ardilla's ray projectors. So The Project will be operated from here.'

'But how could that be possible?' protested the Professor.

'Presently I will show you,' replied Multavo. 'You should not be surprised, because even on Earth, you have told me, your electronic and atomic experts plan to launch more and more ambitious artificial satellites.'

Enlightenment dawned in the Professor's eyes. 'Ah!' he breathed. 'An artificial satellite! I should have guessed it. But that still leaves formidable questions to be answered.'

'Here we were experimenting with artificial satellites long ago,' said Multavo. 'They were not pursued because at that time it was decided they could serve no useful purpose. There were enough satellites in space without making more. The one we shall use on this occasion will be powered by what you call atomic energy. It may be necessary to make several. We shall know that after the first has been launched.'

'What exactly do you intend to do?' asked Rex. 'I'm afraid I'm getting out of my depth.'

'The satellite will circle Ardilla in a continuous orbit, or for as long as we may wish, emitting the reflecting medium.'

'But won't it soon run out of this medium?'

'Never.'

'*Never!*'

'The medium will be produced in endless supply by radio-activity within the satellite. We do not claim that the satellite will remain in its orbit for all eternity, but it should last for as long as is necessary. We could put up more at intervals should they be required. The first one is ready. If it succeeds as well as we hope, it should be enough. It would now be on its way, but we saw you coming so the launching was postponed in case it should affect you. Now you are here we can proceed.'

'This is tremendous news,' declared the Professor. 'I can't imagine how all this was achieved in so short a time.'

'Already possessing the necessary scientific knowledge it was only a matter of working out the constructional details. We have been engaged on The Project since the first reports of Ardilla's activities, and, after all, we are far in advance of Earth in such matters. Your scientists, confronted with the same problem, might have worked out the answer in theory, although it is unlikely that they would have been able to put it in practical form. That is a matter of time. The laws governing the Universe are a vast subject, and you on Earth still have a long way to go; but the day will come when you will know as much about these things as we do.'

Vargo had said little. He had obviously been deep in thought. Now he spoke. 'There are still one or two points I don't understand.'

'What are they?'

'You are going to launch The Project from here?'

'Yes.'

'Towards Ardilla?'

'Yes.'

'At escape velocity?'

'Of course. It would be no use otherwise.'

'But the moment it encounters Ardilla's atmosphere it will become incandescent and disintegrate.'

'It will never reach Ardilla's atmosphere?'

'Why not?'

'It will be stopped.'

'*Stopped*!'

'Perhaps I had better explain. I purposely refrained from

going into the atomic mechnaics of the device because they are highly complicated and not really relevant. The satellite will leave here at a velocity necessary to take it beyond our atmosphere. The velocity, of course, will then automatically increase. Before reaching Ardilla's atmosphere, still being under our control, it will be stopped by putting the jet thrusts into reverse – just as you control your ship. An atomic device will then come into action. This will take it away from Ardilla at orbital velocity. When this is reached all propelling mechanism will stop. Ardilla's gravity will do the rest. The satellite will take up its orbit and continue to circle the planet indefinitely. Only we, by remote control, could stop it. Or, if we wished, we could destroy it.'

'Aren't you afraid Ardilla might spot it, and do that? They must be very advanced in such matters.'

'They might see it, but to stop it would take time, and by then The Project will, or should, have made them helpless. We shall soon know if it is working as planned.'

'How?'

'By the behaviour of Ardilla. No theory can be said to be infallible until it has been tested in practice, but we have done our best. All we can do now is send the satellite on its way and await results. Would you like to see the satellite?'

'I would, very much,' answered the Professor, enthusiastically.

'We are going to the launching ground?' asked Rex.

'Not immediately. There is no need to go there yet. I will first find out if everything is ready. Having seen something of our television, as you call it, on your last visit, this should not surprise you.' So saying Multavo touched a button beside him.

Instantly a large panel in the wall, which Rex recognized as a television screen, began to glow. A picture appeared and came into focus. It showed what looked like an airfield with several men standing in the foreground. Multavo spoke in the native language. One of the men turned and answered. Multavo replied briefly and switched off. The picture faded. He got up. 'Come with me,' he invited.

They returned to the vehicle which had brought them to the house. Multavo took his seat and they glided away. After a journey of some distance they came to an open area, a corner of which Rex recognized as the place he had seen on the television screen. The same men were standing there. Mutavo spoke to them. One opened a gate and they glided through.

In the distance Rex could see a tower. From it an object like a gigantic torpedo was pointing obliquely at the sky. Multavo did not proceed towards it, but turned aside to stop before a large, massive building.

All eyes were on what was obviously the satellite.

'On Earth we should call that a rocket,' said the Professor.

'Or a guided missile,' contributed Tiger.

'One name is as good as another,' said Multavo quietly. 'Come in. There are several things here that should interest you.'

'Is this the control room?' asked the Professor.

'It is rather more than that,' answered Multavo. 'It is one of our main observation stations. I will show you.' He led the way inside.

15 Zero hour

They followed Multavo down a corridor, and presently through an arched entrance that gave access to a large, austere hall, with a floor of some curious rubber-like substance. The ceiling was a dome which gave the place the appearance of an observatory. There were balconies at intervals, reached by spiral stairways. There was electronic apparatus everywhere. At eye level round the walls, inset, were television screens, some dead, others with pictures flashing across them. There were also instruments which looked to Rex like futuristic radar equipment. Operators stood in front of switchboards and panels, watching the pictures.

'This is not an ordinary observation station', explained Multavo. 'Its purpose is not for entertainment but to enable us to see what is going on around us. This, for example, was designed for the special purpose for which it is being used.' He pointed to a screen close at hand across which in swift, regular succession, were passing bars of brilliant light, reminding Rex of interference all too often seen on television screens on Earth.

'What is causing that?' he asked.

Multavo answered, 'Can't you guess? What you see is an Ardilla ray in operation; and although at this distance it is too weak to do us any injury we haven't failed to notice that the influence is steadily becoming stronger, brighter, more definite. Which makes it clear that if we fail to find a remedy the rays will not only be seen, but felt. They could drive us off this planet. That may be the intention. We don't know.'

'Does this interference affect your ordinary radio screens?' asked Rex.

'No. The rays are of a different nature from the common

interference waves. This is not an orthodox instrument. It operates on a different principle, and was, as I have said, designed to pick up and show the Ardilla rays. It was necessary for us to know when they were being transmitted, also their strength.'

'So after your satellite has been launched this instrument will tell you whether or not it has been successful,' said the Professor.

'Exactly. If the rays continue after the satellite has reached its orbit we shall know we have failed. By the way; this may interest you.' Multavo walked over to a box-like compartment set in the wall and opened it. In it was a small lever. 'This is the master switch that will launch the satellite,' he said quietly. 'Would you like to see the satellite depart?'

'I would indeed,' answered the Professor, 'Do you mean see it in reality or on a television screen?'

'Whichever you wish. There will be no danger in watching the real thing. Special observation posts have been made.'

'Capital. Let us watch from one.'

Rex was still thinking of the masterswitch. 'So this was what war could come to,' he pondered. 'One little lever pressed by one man, to put a whole world out of action.'

They all followed Multavo back to the open ground where the fabulous rocket – from its shape Rex could only think of it as a rocket – was waiting. It was a fearful-looking object. Its size, and that of the tower that supported it, gave it a look of awful power. It was more like the nightmare of a deranged scientist than a man-made machine. Yet Rex realized with an uncomfortable thrill of apprehension, the rockets and guided missiles made on Earth were getting larger, more efficient, every year. This, no doubt, was what they would look like in the not very distant future. Even now the only difference was a matter of range. Here was the ultimate version, an interplanetary missile.

Rex suddenly felt sorry for future generations. To be bombarded by rockets based on the same planet was bad enough, but when the time came, when they could arrive from space, without warning, life would hardly be worth living. There would be no peace of mind for anyone.

'Well, that certainly is a rocket,' observed Tiger, admiringly.

'To serve its purpose it could not be made any smaller,' explained Multavo. 'As you will suppose it consists of several compartments, each holding the equipment required for the successive operations.'

'I still think it might become a target for an Ardilla ship,' said Tiger. 'They are bound to have interceptors.'

'We are not afraid of that,' returned Multavo. 'Before they could do anything the protective layer would have formed, and being radioactive it will be indestructible. But the time has come for the launching. As you see, the ground is already being cleared.'

Again they trooped along behind Multavo as he strode towards one of several thick-walled shelters built low in the ground. They entered. The heavy doors were closed. They took their places at a narrow observation slit, filled with an unknown thickness of glass or similar material, which looked out across the now deserted launching ground.

'The switch to start the satellite on its flight will be thrown by the chief engineer in the presence of others concerned with The Project,' said Multavo. 'There is the warning signal,' he went on quickly, as a blue disc in the wall blinked three times. 'Watch, for you are about to witness something which not even we have previously attempted. Until now, of course, we have had no reason to resort to such an experiment as this.'

They waited. Rex, staring through the slit, could feel his heart beating faster. He knew from their expression that the others, too, were conscious of a tension in the air. No one spoke.

Rex flinched as with a roar that seemed to shake the ground on which he stood the satellite began to rise with an awe-inspiring, majestic deliberation. Swiftly gathering speed, within a matter of seconds, for all its size, it was no more than a speck in the sky, with a faint vapour trail to mark its passage. An instant later it had disappeared.

'It has gone,' said Multavo, without emotion, after the reverberations had died down. 'All we can do now is await the result.'

'I'll wager the designer is limp from relief,' murmured Tiger. 'I know the strain of watching an important experiment. I imagine that even here things can sometimes go wrong.'

'Of course,' agreed Multavo. 'We are not infallible.'

'Where will you wait for the result?' inquired the Professor, polishing his spectacles, which had steamed up from perspiration on his forehead.

'From the observation room. We shall see nothing more from here. After the dust has settled we will go there to see if all is well.'

The cloud of dust raised by the satellite was fast dispersing as they walked across the launching ground to the car, which took them back to the interstellar vision station.

After a word with the guard on duty at the door they walked down the corridor to a side room where several elderly men were seated before a particularly large screen. Multavo made a sign of greeting, which was acknowledged, and invited his guests to be seated. Rex's eyes were already on the screen. It showed merely an area of black with a tiny white spot in the centre.

'Is that it?' he whispered.

'Yes,' answered Multavo. He spoke quietly in his own language to one of the men already seated and received a reply. 'All goes well,' he told Rex. 'The satellite has settled on its course. Nothing should go wrong now. However, we will watch it until it fades, which will not be long.'

'I assume it has already left your atmosphere?' whispered the Professor.

'Some time ago. At any moment now it should drop off the launching apparatus, which is no longer needed. We should be able to see it go. Ah! There it is now,' he added quickly, as a second object appeared below the first.

'Is there no risk of it falling on Terromagna?'

'None. Heat by friction will vaporize it before it can reach the ground. That was taken into account, of course.'

After that they sat in silence to watch the satellite fade, leaving the screen blank. One by one the engineers of The Project got up and went out.

'I think we might go, too,' said Multavo, presently. 'We shall see nothing more. The satellite has a long way to go so there will be some delay before anything happens.'

'What will be the next step,' asked the Professor.

'What we hope for it the disappearance on the other screen of the interference caused by Ardilla's lethal rays. If it persists we shall have failed.' Multavo smiled faintly. 'To you this must seem a strange war, but, unhappily, it would be no exaggeration to say that the future of every planet in the galaxy could depend on what happens in the next few hours. We can only wait. There is nothing more for us to do.'

They spent the remainder of the day walking round the great observation station looking at the wonders with which it was equipped, Multavo repeating that they were merely having a preview of their own future; that all these things would one day be just as commonplace on Earth. Some of the instruments were demonstrated and, as on the occasion of their previous visit to Terromagna, they had the staggering experience of watching events on other planets of the Terromagna solar system. Rex asked if they could be shown Earth; but in this he was disappointed, Multavo saying that they had not yet reached that stage of development, although no doubt it would come, if not in his lifetime.

They had a meal and a rest at Multavo's house and then, at an hour which Rex judged must be towards dawn, they made their way back to the Ardilla ray-detector screen, their host telling them that the effect of the satellite, should it be successful, might be expected at any time now.

They found other watchers already assembled in an atmosphere of some anxiety. No one spoke. All eyes were on the screen on which, Rex observed with dismay, the sinister rays still registered.

'They look as strong as ever,' he whispered to Multavo.

'They will be, unless they go entirely. It will be one thing or the other.'

They found seats and prepared to wait.

There were a number of dials on the wall, and presently Rex noticed that it was one of these, not the screen, that most of those present were watching. It was larger than the others, with a face like a clock but with a single hand. This was moving imperceptibly towards the vertical, or twelve o'clock position, marked with a broad red line.

Rex touched Multavo on the arm. 'What is that thing? What's it doing?' he breathed.

'It is merely an instrument for measuring time; not as you know it, of course, but one specially designed to show the passage of The Project,' answered Multavo. 'When the hand reaches the red line the satellite will have arrived at the objective, and, all being well, start on its orbital encirclement of Ardilla.'

'Thank you.' Again Rex settled back to watch, his eyes now on the time counter.

The hand crept on remorselessly, and with it the atmosphere in the chamber became increasingly tense.

Rex found himself thinking thoughts as unreal as his surroundings. So this was how war would ultimately be fought, he brooded. Between worlds, with unseen weapons, victory or defeat being registered on the dial of an instrument. Individuals no longer meant anything. It was either the complete and utter extermination of a planet, or nothing. After what he had already seen he was not as impressed as he would have expected. He realized that his faculty for surprise was slowly but surely being eliminated, as had been predicted.

There was a general stiffening in the attitude of the watchers as the hand of the clock approached zero hour. It reached it. Nothing happened. Rex braced himself for something, although he did not know what. But still nothing happened. The hand passed on. The ray interference still flickered across the screen.

Rex moistened his lips. He looked at Multavo. 'It isn't going to work,' he whispered.

Multavo did not answer. His face was pale. Seconds passed. A minute. Five – ten minutes. Then, with a faint click the hand on the dial flashed back to the needle from which apparently it had started. Simultaneously, after a final flicker, the significant bars of white light on the screen faded, leaving it blank with a pearly opalescence. The scientists and engineers sprang to their feet, and for a little while there was an excited babble of conversation. There were smiles for the visitors. Then the assembly broke up, leaving Multavo and his friends alone.

'I gather that means The Project has worked,' said Tiger.

'It can mean nothing else,' declared Multavo. 'This is the first time, since the rays appeared, that the screen has been blank.'

'Wonderful,' congratulated the Professor.

Even the unimpressionable Multavo seemed moved. 'You realize what this means!' he exclaimed. 'Space travel should once again be safe. You should have no trouble in reaching home. I wonder if our neighbours will appreciate what they owe to us. No doubt they are going about their affairs unaware of the importance of this day. There is no need to stay here any longer. We will return to my home and celebrate with some cups of tea.'

'And I must be getting back to Mino, to tell them the good news,' said Vargo.

They were walking towards the door when from somewhere came a sharp, high-pitched whine.

'Excuse me a moment,' requested Multavo.

They turned. A disc over an imposing instrument was glowing with a red light. One of the operators went to it and listened at what was evidently a sort of amplifier. He looked at Multavo and beckoned.

'Nothing wrong, I hope,' said the Professor, anxiously.

'I don't know. It is an interplanetary radio call, so it may be news of the satellite,' answered Multavo, walking towards the instrument.

'Where is it coming from? Do you know?'

'No. But I soon will.'

Reaching the instrument Multavo began making adjustments by turning some controls not unlike those commonly used on Earth for the control of electrical devices. The whine, and the red light, waxed and waned as he did so. Then, suddenly, a voice was speaking. What it said Rex did not understand; but judging from the expression of incredulity on his face, Vargo did.

'That is Rolto speaking,' he translated.

'Rolto!' cried the Professor. 'Speaking from where?'

'I don't know. But it must be from somewhere clear of the influence of the satellite. Listen. Quiet, please.'

In a hush that was profound the voice from space continued. Rex, who knew a certain amount of Minoese, caught a word here and there. He gathered that the same message was being repeated. Then the voice stopped. The red light went out. Vargo and Multavo stared at each other with expressions that provoked Rex's curiosity. Multavo's face relaxed gradually to a smile.

'What was all that about?' inquired the Professor.

'We have won the war against Ardilla. The satellite has done even more than was hoped of it.'

Vargo answered. 'I will tell you. Rolto was a prisoner on Ardilla. He thought we might be here. He was acting as an official spokesman for Ardilla.'

'But what was the message?'

'He says the people of Ardilla are in a state of panic. Many are ill, having lost the use of their limbs. Something has gone wrong with their ray-casting machines and they believe Terromagna to have been responsible. Rolto first tried to get a message through from Ardilla, but found it impossible. Of course, he was not to know that our barrier would stop it. At the time nothing was known of our satellite.'

'Well?'

'So Ardilla released him, with his ship, to make contact with us, only he being able to speak our language. In a word, Ardilla is asking Terromagna to stop whatever it is doing. In return, they promise never again to use their ray weapons. Not that they would be of any use if they did use them. They are no longer effective.'

'So what has happened is what was planned in The Project.'

'Without doubt. Their rays are rebounding back on them from the artificial layer that now surrounds them.'

'It will destroy them!'

'Certainly if they persist with their rays they will destroy themselves. We may suppose they were in a panic when they realized that they have only to switch off their rays for the bombardment of their planet to cease.'

'You could have told Rolto that in case it had not been realized.'

'The time lag makes a two-way conversation impossible. I could answer the message now and it would be received tomorrow by our time. But I have no authority to act on my own account. All I can do is report this to the Council of Elders.'

'What will they do?' asked the Professor. 'It would be a terrible thing to liquidate all life on Ardilla.'

'We shall not do that.'

'What could you do?'

'We can destroy the satellite or divert it from its present orbit into infinite space.'

'Even so, the layer it has laid would remain.'

'For a time. After a while it would disperse. Meanwhile, the people of Ardilla will come to no harm now that the rays have been cut off, as we know they have been, from the screen. No doubt the paralysing effects will wear off as they did with you.'

'Did you think Ardilla is to trusted not to resume the attack when it realizes the barrage has gone?' queried Tiger, dubiously.

'Yes. Not being fools they will realize that if we can send one satellite we can dispatch others. They have learned a lesson, which is that our counter-weapon is more powerful than their ray, which we can cause to recoil upon them. I am sure they will be more careful in future. But come. I must report to the Council. You can wait for me at my house, if you will.'

'With pleasure,' agreed the Professor.

Multavo took them home, and leaving them there went on to the Council Chamber. He was away about an hour. When he returned he was able to announce the Council's decision.

'A message is being sent to Ardilla, via Rolto, regretting any casualties they may have had, although these were not caused so much by us as by their rays. We had to protect ourselves. We have no designs on them or their planet. They are advised to adopt the same policy. If they will refrain from sending out any more harmful rays, we, for our part, will put out no more satellites and destroy the one that now threatens them.'

'Nothing could be more fair,' asserted the Professor.

'Now that travel is again safe we have many things to do,' went on Multavo. Someone will have to go to Dacoona to see what has happened there to account for their silence. If the people have recovered from the effects of the rays, or whatever it was that beset them, we shall proceed with our investigations in the field of an extended life span.'

'Rolto must have had an experience he is not likely to forget,' remarked Vargo. 'It may have cured him of the persecution complex from which he has for some time suffered.'

'He is the one man who appeared to resent our intrusion into your society,' said the Professor, sadly.

'He should be sent to us for treatment; we could cure him,' advised Multavo. He looked around. 'What would you like to do next? I hope you will be able to stay with me for a little while longer.'

'We must leave for home tomorrow,' decided Vargo. 'Our purpose in making this voyage has been achieved and the High Council will be anxious to have a full report on the matter.'

'As you will,' agreed Multavo. 'I shall not come with you because, as you know, my work is here. Tonight we can sleep in peace. Tomorrow, without fear of Ardilla, you can start for home with confidence.'

'As long as the Professor doesn't want to do any more exploring on the way,' said Tiger, slyly.

'No,' denied the Professor, firmly. 'I have seen enough for one voyage. Now I look forward to a quiet time at home, where I shall be able to devote my thoughts to the wonders I have seen.'

'I think that goes for all of us,' put in Toby.

They all agreed.